# REVOLUTION OF AIR & RUST

# DAVID LEE SUMMERS
# REVOLUTION OF AIR & RUST

Hadrosaur Productions, Mesilla Park, NM

Revolution of Air and Rust
Hadrosaur Productions
First Edition, first printing, continuous printing on demand
First date of publication: November 2012
Author: David Lee Summers, www.davidleesummers.com
Cover Art: Laura Givens, www.lauragivens-artist.com

ISBN: 1-885093-66-7

Hadrosaur Productions
P.O. Box 2194
Mesilla Park, NM 88047-2194
www.hadrosaur.com

Other books in the
**Empires of Steam and Rust** Series:

*Gateway to Rust and Ruin* by Robert E. Vardeman
*Heart of Steam and Rust* by Stephen D. Sullivan
*Unforeseen: Journey Through Rust and Ruin*
by Sarah Bartsch


Other books by David Lee Summers:

**Old Star/New Earth Series**
*The Solar Sea*
*The Pirates of Sufiro*
*Children of the Old Stars*
*Heirs of the New Earth*

**Scarlet Order Vampire Series:**
*Vampires of the Scarlet Order*
*Dragon's Fall: Rise of the Scarlet Order*

**Legacy of the Dead Series:**
*The Astronomer's Crypt*

**Clockwork Legion Series:**
*Owl Dance*
*Lightning Wolves*
*The Brazen Shark*

**Science Fiction Anthologies:**
*A Kepler's Dozen*
*Space Pirates*
*Space Horrors*

# REVOLUTION OF AIR & RUST

# Chapter One

It was a quiet morning as the sun rose over Cuauhtémoc in the Mexican state of Chihuahua. Umberto Mondragón ate a thin, corn-masa porridge called atole and sipped a rare, precious cup of coffee as he prepared for work at the corner grocery where he made tortillas. The quiet was broken by a dog barking up the street followed by a loud, authoritative voice. Although Umberto couldn't make out the words, he thought someone must be shouting orders. He became conscious of a low thrumming sound. Umberto set his coffee cup down and went to the door.

Two children in the street, holding a stick and a ball stared upward as a shadow eclipsed the sun. Umberto followed their gaze and saw an airship. The thrumming sound came from its engines. On its flank was a white star within a blue circle. The American Expeditionary Force had arrived.

A half dozen men in crisp, khaki uniforms turned the corner onto Umberto's street. They wore tall, wide-brimmed Montana hats. Three of them turned east, away from Umberto's door while the rest marched his direction. One of them pounded on the first door they came to. When no one answered, they moved on to the next door. The two boys with the stick and ball scurried down the street, away from the American soldiers.

Spying Umberto, one of the soldiers pointed. "You there," he shouted in English. Switching to heavily accented Spanish, he said, "We want information about Pancho Villa. We will pay." He rubbed his fingers together, as though fondling crisp, American greenbacks.

Before Umberto could speak, a gunshot thundered through the quiet morning, shattering glass and winging one of the American soldiers. He fell back against an adobe wall, while his comrades turned their attention to the house where the shot had come from.

There was a cry of "Viva la revolución!" and another gunshot. One of the soldiers kicked in the door. Umberto scrambled back inside, slamming his own door. He didn't know what scared him more, the American Expeditionary Force that occupied Northern Mexico, Villa's revolutionaries, or President Carranza's Federal soldiers.

Umberto made the sign of the cross as he heard more shouts and gunshots. Soon afterward, it grew eerily quiet. After a moment, he stepped back over to the table and lifted the coffee cup to his lips with a trembling hand. A pounding at the door startled him and he sloshed the coffee over his shirt.

Returning to the door, Umberto peered outside. The American soldier who had shouted at him earlier stood there. His hat had fallen back, held around his neck by the chinstrap, revealing disheveled, sandy hair. "Pancho Villa—do you know where he is?"

Umberto shook his head. "His men were all around town when I came home last night. They were in the cantinas raising a ruckus. I thought they would be sleeping off their hangovers this morning." He shrugged. "But, if they knew you were coming, they may have left."

The soldier grimaced. "Who's harboring them? Where are they staying?"

Umberto swirled his gnarled finger through the air. "All over. Many sympathize with the revolution."

"Your neighbor?" The soldier inclined his head in the direction of the skirmish up the street.

Umberto wondered what had happened to the man, but nodded. "Yes, a few of Villa's men were in that house."

The soldier grimaced. "Well, they're not there now. Where could they have gone?"

"If they left during the night, they could be halfway to Madera by now."

"Hiding in rugged terrain." The soldier nodded. He turned to leave, but stopped and retrieved some pesos from his pocket.

Umberto took them and sighed, the pesos weren't as valuable as greenbacks, but they were safer. He hadn't really betrayed any secrets—he had no secrets to betray—but he had heard many stories of what Pancho Villa did to those who opposed him.

"And how exactly does that help us?"

"Black Jack Pershing has a much weaker force up here in the North. He just has to 'stabilize' Sonora and Chihuahua. If we focus our attacks on Pershing and drive him out, the American line in the middle of the country will be vulnerable from the rear as well as the front. We'd stand a much better chance of driving the Americans out altogether." Villa shrugged. "I'm not especially fond of Venustiano Carranza, but I could learn to work with him if he felt he owed me a debt of gratitude."

Fierro shook his head slowly. "So, all we have to do is defeat Black Jack Pershing when our back's against the wall and we're nearly out of supplies." He poured another shot of tequila into his glass. "Even Álvaro Obregón has gone over to Pershing's side."

"Obregón's nothing. He just thinks Teddy Roosevelt will make him a governor if the northern states of Mexico are annexed by America. Most of his men are easily bought."

"All right, so what exactly do we do?"

Villa looked up and saw that Maria was loitering a short distance away with a coat over her arm. He gathered her shift must be over. He poured one last shot of tequila and lifted the glass. "Tonight, I will pray for guidance and you will send some of our men along the roads to find out exactly how we're hemmed in. Maybe we can find a weakness to exploit."

Fierro touched his glass to Villa's and they drank together. Pancho Villa stood steadily despite the alcohol he'd consumed and walked over to Maria, holding out his arm. She linked her arm around his and they left for the church.

# Chapter Two

General John J. Pershing entered the dining room of the house he occupied in Ciudad Chihuaha. A long table was covered with maps, charts and reports. Officers examined the papers and spoke quietly among themselves. A moment later, they realized the general had entered the room and all snapped to attention, saluting. Pershing returned the salute. "As you were, gentlemen."

The officers resumed their work as the general's adjutant, Major Clarence Burton stepped forward, shaking his head. "I don't know how he does it, but Villa saw us coming again."

"He knows the countryside and he has many friends." Pershing pursed his lips. The general once counted himself among Francisco "Pancho" Villa's friends. But that was before President Roosevelt ordered Pershing and the 8th Brigade across the border to stabilize Northern Mexico and keep the revolution from spilling into the United States.

"We have friends, too," protested Major Burton.

Pershing nodded. "Indeed we do, and I plan to take advantage of that fact." He looked at his wrist watch. "General Obregón will be here shortly. Show him to my office when he arrives."

"Yes, sir," said Burton, snapping a salute.

Pershing returned the salute, then continued through the dining room into the study he used as an office. The large house served his needs well. Crossing to a window, he looked outside and saw a newly completed wall topped with barbed wire. The garrison was making excellent progress securing the neighborhood they occupied. Chihuahua was a nice enough city despite the revolution and he hoped he could bring his wife and children down from San Francisco, soon. Before that happened, he wanted Pancho Villa in custody. That was all that remained to assure him and the president that the mission was complete.

He sat down and began reading through a sheaf of papers he found on the desk. His men had determined that Villa had fled into the mountains above Cuauhtémoc. He pulled out a map and studied the villages, roads, and terrain, trying to decide where he would go and what he would do if he were in Villa's position.

The general's thoughts were interrupted by a knock at the door. "Come in," he called.

Major Burton entered and held the door open. "General Obregón to see you, sir."

General Álvaro Obregón strode through the door. Approaching Pershing's desk, he removed his hat and held out his hand. Pershing clasped it, then indicated a chair. "May I offer you a drink, General. Coffee, perhaps?"

"Most gracious, General. Coffee would be fine. Thank you."

Pershing looked over to Major Burton and nodded, indicating that he should make it so.

The adjutant nodded in reply, then closed the door behind him.

"My men report that the Villistas are now in Madera," said Obregón as Pershing took his seat.

"I guessed that." He sighed. "The problem is, if we march there, he'll vanish into the mountains until he eventually turns up somewhere else. We need to adjust our strategy. I'd like him to stay put long enough to get comfortable, use up some of his supplies."

Obregón nodded. "I see. The mountains are formidable, but his men can escape that way more easily than you can pursue."

"Exactly. I'd like to keep him hemmed in, but if I tighten the noose too much, he'll just slip through."

There was a knock at the door. "Come in," called Pershing. A sergeant entered with a porcelain carafe and cups on a silver tray. As he poured two cups of coffee, Pershing studied the Mexican general. Obregón was something of a mystery to him. At one point, he had been a revolutionary just like Villa, although Pershing gathered there had been disagreements about tactics. Obregón preferred to fight battles with overwhelming numbers of infantry while Villa preferred intense cavalry charges.

Perhaps that difference explained why Obregón helped the Americans while Villa fought them. Obregón was a revolutionary because he wanted stability as well as equal rights for workers. The Americans brought that. Villa was a revolutionary because he wanted to break the control of the big hacienda owners—or at least that's what he said. The truth was Villa didn't see himself as subservient to anyone, whether it was land owners, President Carranza, or the American Expeditionary Force.

Pershing sipped his coffee, then set the cup aside and retrieved the map of Northern Mexico. "There are only a few roads out of Madera. I have a strong force in Cuauhtémoc. I could move some of my people into La Junta and Guererro. Could you spare some men for Buenaventura?" That would put the weak link on the long road to Ciudad Chihuahua—just where Pershing wanted it.

Obregón frowned. "I don't have many men, General Pershing, but I'll see what I can do."

"That's all I ask." Pershing gave the former revolutionary a reassuring grin.

Rodolfo Fierro sat on the porch of a rooming house in Madera, smoking a cigarette and watching clouds drift over the mountains. Pancho Villa had taken a house closer to the center of town, but he spent an increasing amount of time at the boarding house where Maria Reyes lived. He emerged wearing his finest jacket and a cravat, just as Fierro lit his third cigarette. An almost cherubic smile lit Villa's features and he held out his hands. "Isn't it a beautiful morning, Rodolfo?"

Fierro took out his pocket watch. "It's nearly noon."

Villa waved his hand through the air, as though clearing away both his friend's objections and the cigarette smoke. "Come and walk with me." He left the porch with Fierro following close on his heels.

"So, do you plan to marry this one?"

"Depends on how long we stay." Villa shrugged. "This would be a nice place to make a home, but I wonder if she would remain behind very long after we leave."

"Why do you say that?"

"She says she lost her family in the fighting at Zacatecas and she's looking to start a new life."

"We're a long way from Zacatecas." Fierro narrowed his gaze. "I'm surprised a young woman alone was able to travel that far."

Villa stopped and looked at Fierro. "Are you suggesting she has another … companion?"

Fierro took a drag on his cigarette and blew the smoke out. "All I suggest is that you be careful."

"All women should be handled with care," said Villa with a grin. "So, I don't think you were loitering on the porch to consult with me about my love life." He resumed his walk down the street. "What have our people learned?"

"They've been counting Pershing's men. Most of his force is divided between Cuauhtémoc, Guerrero and La Junta. Obregón has a small force in Buenaventura. We could buy them off and go to Ciudad Juárez and restock supplies."

"How many men does Black Jack have guarding his compound in Chihuahua?"

"Not many, if the counts are accurate. Also, he's using his two airships as sentries, patrolling the roads out of Madera." Fierro shook his head. "It's only a matter of time before he calls in reinforcements from the north—strengthens his position in Chihuahua and starts to move in on us here."

"From what you tell me, I see two choices. We can go to Juárez where we can resupply easily, but will give Pershing time to bolster his force or—" a slow grin spread across Pancho Villa's face "—we could take the attack to Pershing now."

Fierro dropped the cigarette butt to the ground and stomped it out. "I don't like it, Pancho. It seems too easy."

Villa stopped and put his hand on Fierro's shoulder. "We know most of Pershing's men are away from Chihuahua. Even if he gets word that we've left Madera, he's going to wonder which way we went. He'll split up his forces. Even if he brings them all back to Chihuahua, we know where they're coming from. If we find ourselves outnumbered, we escape. We can still go to Juárez."

Fierro pursed his lips, but nodded. "Yes, that makes sense. When do you want to leave?"

"Let's give ourselves a couple more days so the men and

horses are well rested." Villa chuckled at an inner thought. "Maybe by then, I'll have decided whether I want to ask Maria Reyes to marry me or not."

# Chapter Three

It took a week for Pancho Villa's men to wind their way through arroyos and skirt back roads to a makeshift camp in the foothills across the Sacramento River from Ciudad Chihuahua. General John J. Pershing and his officers occupied a neighborhood adjoining the small mountain called Cerro del Coronel. Hastily constructed wooden structures dotted the bare land around the mountain. Some were barracks for enlisted men. Some were garages for the trucks used by Pershing's cavalry. Some held the munitions and supplies Villa hoped to capture while Pershing's men patrolled the roads out of Madera. Atop the mountain were mooring towers for the American airships. Just a few guards patrolled the encampment's perimeter.

It was perfect. Villa's cavalry could charge in, get the equipment and supplies they needed, and ride out again before General Pershing could summon his forces back from Cuauhtémoc.

Sitting in his tent, Villa looked at his pocket watch by the light of a lantern. It was 9 PM. If his sources were correct, General Pershing, along with most of the men who remained at the encampment would be bedding down soon. Only the perimeter guards would remain. What's more, the moon would be rising soon, affording his men enough light to see their targets. It was time to get the men to their horses.

Villa summoned Rodolfo Fierro who passed word to the officers—letting them know it was time to assemble the troops. Meanwhile, Villa donned two bandoliers of ammunition along with a pith helmet that he secured with a leather strap. Within the hour, horsemen formed up ranks and began riding toward Pershing's encampment. The moon rose as Pancho Villa spurred his horse into the Sacramento River. Once the entire force had crossed, the officers sent men to their assigned positions and pointed out their targets.

Pancho Villa unsheathed his machete and held it high. "Viva la revolución!" With that, the cavalrymen charged toward their targets. Shots rang out as mounted marksmen and perimeter guards exchanged fire.

As the horses surged forward, a row of electric lights flared to life ahead and to the left. A half dozen Ford flatbed trucks had been tucked out of sight, among the buildings of Chihuahua. They crossed the path of the cavalry charge. Villa realized all too late what the trucks were doing. He watched helpless as the first line of mounted men rushed into rolls of barbed wire laid down by men riding on the truck beds. The horses tumbled and fell, spilling their riders. A moment later, he flew over his horse's head and felt a numbing pain in his face and tasted dirt and blood in his mouth.

Painfully, he pushed himself to his feet. Around him was a cacophony of braying. Confused horses with broken and cut limbs tried to free themselves of the barbed wire. The men fared little better. Some lay on the ground, howling at the pain of broken limbs. Some were still, either from split skulls or broken necks. A few others pushed themselves to their feet.

Villa swore. This was a trick opposing generals had used on him before, but it was the first time the barbed wire had been deployed at the last minute by trucks. Still, the men were prepared and carried tools to deal with such a contingency. He spit dirt and a broken tooth from his mouth. "Wire cutters," he called. "And be careful."

He took a moment to scan the ground for the machete he lost when he fell. Not seeing it, he pulled his six-gun and checked that it was loaded. Looking back to the river, he saw Fierro sitting astride his horse, shouting orders to his men. At least they had seen what was happening and stopped in time. The men dismounted and donned tools.

Meanwhile, those men with Villa pushed forward through the rows of barbed wire. Villa wondered how Pershing knew about the cavalry charge. It was certainly possible some of his men were spotted as they approached Chihuahua, but the trucks had been lying in wait as though Pershing had guessed details of the attack known only to a few of his most trusted men until the charge commenced. Was there a spy in his ranks? If so, who was it?

Villa shook the thoughts aside. He had a battle to win. Even if Pershing had garnered enough information from a spy to know when he planned to attack, there was no way he had time to summon enough men to mount a successful defense.

His men breeched the second row of barbed wire and rushed ahead to the third. The ranks behind had also succeeded in clearing a path through the wire.

Just as Villa began to wonder what had happened to the cavalry trucks, he heard a thrumming sound and his heart sank further.

From behind Cerro del Coronel, an airship climbed into the sky. Moonlight glinted from the fabric of the gasbag. An electric light flared to life just forward of the gondola. Shielding his eyes from the bright light, Villa could just make out a pair of electrodes descending from the gondola's keel.

Once they were fully deployed, electrical energy arced between the two electrodes and soon whirled into a fierce, glowing sphere of energy. The electrodes flared blue for a moment and the lightning ball was hurled at a knot of men to Villa's left. The men were vaporized where they stood, leaving only a black scorch mark on the ground and melted barbed wire.

Villa turned and ran to his right. He heard the roar of a truck engine. Looking around, he saw a break in the barbed wire cut by his men and he turned back toward the river. The truck rushed past where he had been standing, forcing many of his men into the barbed wire. He put his hands over his ears to shut out the screams. He didn't know how to help them and he realized he had lost this battle. His focus changed from salvaging a victory to leading a successful retreat.

He looked around and tried to catch the eyes of as many men as possible. Fierro knelt near one of the wire coils, firing at the retreating trucks. Villa waved his arms, signaling for his men to return to the camp across the river. Fierro stood and looked around. Catching sight of Villa, he nodded and began shouting orders to his troops.

The thrumming sound grew louder. At first, Villa thought the airship was about to make another pass. Then, he looked across the river and saw flames rising from his encampment. A second airship approached from the foothills. Its light swept the battlefield for targets.

Villa believed Pershing could have assembled the trucks if he had seen his men gathering in the foothills, but there was no way the American general could have summoned both airships without advanced knowledge of the attack. The only people with that kind of knowledge were a handful of generals who had gathered around a small table in the back of a cantina in Madera a week earlier. Fierro, Robles, Talamantes ... who else had been there?

He shook his head as he caught sight of a fork-like pair of electrodes hanging from the second airship's gondola. There was no more time to consider spies; he needed to find cover. The light from the airship's spotlight found him. He rushed out of it, only to have a second spotlight land on him as well. Both airships were in range. He dove out of the way just as both of them fired lightning balls at him.

The two lightning balls collided with an explosion that knocked Villa flat on his ass. He looked up, blinking back the spots before his eyes. One large, deep orange spot refused to vanish. Looking away, he saw the night, the barbed wire, trucks driving down the lines between the coils, injured horses, and his men retreating. Looking up into the sky, he saw the airships making long, lazy arcs. Every few seconds, one would hurtle a lighting ball at the ground. The air was filling with dust, smoke and the smell of charred flesh. The airships would soon be back in position to fire on him again.

Turning his gaze forward, the bright orange void was still there. Squinting, he realized he could make out more detail. It was as though he were looking through a tunnel into another place. The ground was orange sand, not unlike the sand he stood on aside from the color. The sky was painted in swaths of blood red and deep purple, like a smoke-laden sunset. There was a mountain, not unlike Cerro del Coronel. Beyond it was a city, but the buildings were nothing like those of Chihuahua. Instead of adobe houses and the beautiful cathedral, he saw monolithic structures of brick that reminded him of America's factories in the northeast.

Villa looked down and saw that he was bathed in white light again. The airships had completed their arcs and the guns were charging. Without conscious thought, Pancho Villa dove for the tunnel. There was a tremendous sucking sensation and Villa thought he would be pulled apart. A moment later he collapsed in a heap on the strange, orange soil.

There was a bright flash behind him as the lightning balls impacted the ground where he had been. Sand and debris flew over his head and he scrambled away, then turned and sat up. He found he had a difficult time catching his breath. He looked up into the strange, dark sky, pleased to see no airships pursuing him. With some effort, he rose to his feet and took several halting steps toward the place he had been standing just a moment before.

There was no tunnel leading back to the battlefield.

# Chapter Four

Pancho Villa tried to figure out where he was. He had jumped into a tunnel of some kind, but the sun—albeit watery and bloated—rose above the horizon, so he wasn't underground. A riverbed stood before him and hills rose beyond, not unlike the place where he camped the night before. But the river was dry and there was no sign of his encampment or Pershing's. Even though the terrain was familiar, this could not be the Sacramento River.

Thinking of the river, he realized he was thirsty. He holstered his six-gun and unclasped a one-quart canteen from his belt and took a swallow. The coppery taint of blood followed the water down his throat. He felt around his mouth with his tongue and discovered the gap where he'd lost a tooth. He took another drink of water, then put the canteen back on his belt. There was no way to know how long it would be before he found fresh water.

Villa turned his mind to the problem of getting back to the battle. The tunnel, doorway, or whatever it was had seemingly hung in mid-air, or did he imagine that? Perhaps it really was some kind of tunnel. If so, the place where he came through must be nearby—perhaps on the rise across the riverbed. He took a breath of the dusty air and realized it had a metallic taint, not unlike the blood he swallowed. Brow creased, he studied the land that rose before him. The blast he felt must have collapsed whatever tunnel he came through. He walked across the dry streambed and up the opposite bank. He looked around for a tunnel or a cave, but all he found was solid rock. There wasn't even any cactus or grass sprouting through the rocks. There was no sign of a tunnel, or even the debris from a collapsed tunnel.

Shaking his head, Villa climbed to the top of the rise and peered into the distance. The land rose beyond. If there was a battle in that direction, it was further than he could see. Surely he hadn't fallen that far along a tunnel. Even if he did, how could the blast from the airship have collapsed the whole thing so completely?

Villa took another drink from his canteen and considered his options. Logically, he must have come from the direction he faced and there was no way he could be far from the battle. Despite that, the evidence of his eyes told him there was a long stretch of high, barren desert in front of him. He felt the weight of the canteen and realized a quart of water wasn't going to take him far.

Following the streambed was another option, but that didn't seem any more promising. Standing on high ground as he was, he should be able to see airships hovering in the distance and they simply weren't there. That left only one option open, the strange city of brick. At least if he went there, he would have a chance of figuring out where exactly he was.

He struck out, back down the hillside, across the streambed, toward the city. As he walked, he realized he heard no birds. No insects flitted in front of his nose and mouth looking for moisture. It was like seeing the effects of a severe drought. The air was deathly still and as the sun rose higher in the sky, sweat beaded on his forehead. At least the air was dry enough, the sweat evaporated before it ran down his face.

As Villa drew closer to the city, he realized it was larger than his first impression. The buildings tended to be red brick or stone—definitely more like industrial cities on the East Coast of the United States or in England than any city he knew from the Mexican Frontera.

As he passed the first, outlying buildings, he saw that some had windows, but the glass was shattered, broken out of the frames. Some buildings still had signs, but he couldn't make out the words—even the letters were unfamiliar. His brow creased. He knew English, Spanish and even some French and German, but he didn't recognize this. Perhaps it was Greek or Russian.

The wooden door hung askew on one building he passed. He peered inside and could make out metal machines on a concrete floor. He recognized lathes, drill presses, and milling machines. It was a shop for metal work. He turned around and put his hands on his hips. He needed to figure out where he was. If there was someone on the streets, he could ask, but as far as he could tell, the city was abandoned. What he needed was a library, or maybe a city office. Even if he was in a town where they spoke an unfamiliar language, a library might have books in Spanish or English. A city office would have the name written in enough places he hoped he could make some sense out of the alphabet and figure out where he was.

He proceeded down the street and felt strangely relieved to see some slightly less imposing buildings. He saw a small, structure that could have been a corner market, except when he looked inside, all the shelves were bare. Some other buildings nearby might have been houses. In front of some of the buildings were the shells and frames of automobiles, gradually rusting away. Villa wondered how they could be rusting in such dry air.

Eventually, Villa came to a wide road that appeared to be a major thoroughfare through the city. A short distance away, he saw a stone building with lions guarding steps that led to the front door. That seemed promising. As he walked toward the building he felt increasingly like someone was watching him. He looked around but didn't see anyone. As he climbed the steps, he heard a voice from the street.

"Stop right there. Put your hands up and turn around slowly."

Villa did as he was told. On the street was a thin boy, wearing a tweed jacket. Some kind of leather mask covered his mouth and nose with tubes running to a flat, backpack-like device. He wore goggles and a tweed hat. In his hand was a strange gun decorated with brass. Instead of a barrel, there was a glass cylinder that glowed an eerie blue. In front was an electrode, like those on the airships, only smaller. A few weeks ago, Villa would have laughed at the strange gun, but he'd seen what the airship electrodes had done to his men.

"Who are you? Where do you come from?" asked the boy.

"I am ... Francisco Villa. I'm trying to figure out where I am so I can get back home. I came to this place from Ciudad Chihuahua."

"This *is* Chihuahua."

Villa shook his head. "That's impossible. I know Chihuahua well."

The boy lifted his goggles with one hand, while keeping the electrode gun aimed at Villa. He narrowed his deep, brown eyes. "Did you fall through one of the portals?"

"I came through some kind of tunnel, but it collapsed behind me. I wasn't able to find my way back."

The boy was silent, apparently contemplating what to do next.

"Look, if this is Chihuhua," said Villa, "surely you know about the American invasion."

"Invasion?" asked the boy, his eyes widening in shock.

"Yes, Americans with their airships and their electrode guns." Villa waved his hand around in a circle over his head. "That's how I got here. They fired at me and that was when I saw the tunnel."

The boy nodded slowly. "Very interesting. I'd like to hear more."

"Must we talk out here on the steps with your gun pointed at me and my hands in the air?"

"I don't know if I trust you yet, but we can go inside." The boy indicated the doors with his gun. Villa turned around and climbed the remaining stairs. The doors at the top were unlocked. The building was, indeed, a library, but it was in disarray. He entered a grand reading room with a wooden floor. Dust-covered books were scattered on the desks. Chairs were scattered about, some toppled over. A black, wrought-iron spiral staircase ascended to the upper floors of the library. Looking over to the shelves that lined the room, Villa saw the books were in similar disarray. Strangely, there were no cobwebs, as though all the spiders had died long ago and the webs themselves had collapsed.

Villa also noticed the hum of some kind of machinery and the air seemed fresher and easier to breathe.

The boy entered the library and passed Villa. "Follow me."

They proceeded through the stacks of books until they came to an inner office. There were two chairs and a cot. Several cans of food were stacked atop a desk. The boy took off his hat, freeing long hair that ran past the neck. He slipped off the mask and backpack, then removed the coat. A grin slowly spread across Pancho Villa's face. Not a boy after all, but a young woman.

"I told you my name," said Villa. "Perhaps you can tell me yours."

She turned. "I am Alethea Seton." Although Villa heard

the words clearly and distinctly, her mouth did not move. She smiled. "It's called telepathy. You're hearing my thoughts in your mind."

Villa dropped into one of the wooden chairs. He thought about how clearly he'd heard her when she stood at the bottom of the stone steps, even though she wore a leather mask. "So, you can read my thoughts. Can I read yours?"

"You must be able to," she said, "or else you wouldn't understand me." She kept the gun leveled on him as she sat down in the room's other chair. "I hardly know you, Mr. Villa. You will behave like a gentleman, or you will find out what this gun is capable of."

Pancho Villa removed his pith helmet and wiped the sweat from his brow. "What have I done?"

"You were fantasizing about my breasts in your hands. I will thank you to keep those images to yourself."

Villa's mouth fell open, shocked at the candid words of this strange woman. After a moment, he closed his mouth and pursed his lips. He leaned forward and narrowed his gaze. "I can only hear when you speak to me, I don't see as deeply into your mind as you can see into mine."

She snorted. "Your thoughts weren't very deep." She set the gun in her lap and smirked. "Neither are the thoughts about your men and the battle you were fighting." She paused and nodded thoughtfully.

"Where are we really?"

"We really are in Chihuahua City, but it would seem this Mexico has had a somewhat different history than your Mexico..." Her words faded and her eyes glazed over for a moment. "So many turning points..."

Villa's hand eased back toward his holster. Suddenly Alethea was alert, her gun aimed right between his eyes.

"My only thought is to ... level the playing field," said Villa.

"I know," she said. "But I don't want it level. I'm in charge here." She pointed at his holster with her gun. "Take the gun out slowly and drop it to the floor."

He considered for a moment whether he could draw the weapon faster than she could fire, but seeing her finger tighten on the trigger, he realized she had read that thought. With a sigh, he did as she instructed.

Alethea aimed at the six-gun on the ground and fired. There was a bright flash of light, the sharp smell of hot metal, and the gun leapt from the floor as the powder in the cartridges exploded. Pancho Villa blinked until he could see clearly again. Curious, he reached down to touch his ruined six-gun but pulled back his hand with a yelp. He swallowed as though contemplating a severed body part. A moment later, he looked up. "All right, you're in charge. What's next?"

She smiled slowly. "Although you're a cretin, Mr. Villa, you have a noble cause. I see disturbing images in your mind, but I think you actually have something of a good heart. If you'll keep your impulses under control, I think we might be able to help each other."

# Chapter Five

"The only help I need are directions back home," said Villa.

Alethea smirked. "I think I know where you came from, but getting there is going to be something of a challenge." She stood and motioned for Villa to follow. Stepping back into the cavernous reading room and grabbing a pair of binoculars from the librarian's desk, she then ascended the spiral staircase to the top. There, she climbed out onto a short catwalk that led to a short ladder. Standing on that, she pushed open a trapdoor to the roof, letting in the orange light and stale air from outside. She disappeared through the trapdoor and Villa followed.

Emerging onto the roof, Villa found he had a difficult time breathing again, but he had an excellent view of this strange city Alethea called Chihuahua. The landscape was similar to his adopted home town, but not identical. He could make out the Sacramento River's course and he saw the rugged, inverted cone of Cerro Grande. From this side, he saw a deep, crater-like indentation in the summit of Cerro del Coronel, as though some-one had scooped away part of the mountain. The Rio Chuviscar was missing altogether.

Getting his bearings, he realized that the library was strad-dling the course of the missing river. He considered the engi-neering needed to make that happen. What would happen in times of flood? Then he snorted and reminded himself that he was not in Chihuahua and this little gringa was crazy. Or was she a gringa? In spite of her name, she could pass for a peasant girl in any of the Northern Mexican villages he frequented.

"Race is not the issue, Mr. Villa. Culture is. Mexico is the only country I've known."

"Would you please quit doing that?" snarled Villa.

"What?" Aletha turned around with wide, innocent eyes.

"Answering questions I haven't asked aloud."

She tapped her forehead. "Telepathy, remember. Your question came across as clear as if you'd spoken it aloud. I can't necessarily tell the difference unless I'm looking right at you." She shrugged. "You'll find the telepathy comes in handy out here. You'll breathe less, take in less of the rust."

Villa frowned, but nodded. "All right then," he tried thinking. "You told me you'd show me the way back home."

Alethea nodded and led him to the edge of the building, pointing to the northwest. Villa saw a circular patch of blue in the sky. She handed him the binoculars. With them, he could see a distinct circle of blue in the sky with just a wisp of white cloud traversing the middle. It looked normal compared to the red and purple sky surrounding it.

"What is it?" Villa forgot the telepathy and spoke the words aloud.

"It's a portal to another world," said Alethea. "I think it leads to your world."

"And how do we get there?" Villa shook his head. "It must be hundreds of feet in the air! We'd need an airship!"

"Well, some kind of aircraft, and that's where I think we can help each other."

Villa's brow knitted and she motioned for him to follow her back inside. "If we're going to spend much time outside, you're going to need some equipment." Alethea descended the spiral staircase. Reaching the bottom, she went through a door behind the librarian's desk and continued down a set of wooden stairs that led into the basement. The sound of machinery was much louder here, and it was accompanied by the sound of running water.

They came out into a tunnel tiled in a white and blue checkerboard pattern. Dirty water flowed into a machine that straddled a channel in the floor.

"The Rio Chuviscar?" asked Villa.

"What's left of it," affirmed Alethea silently. She pointed to the machine. "This extracts oxygen from the water and feeds it to the building."

Villa nodded. "That's why it's easier to breathe in the library."

"My grandfather built it. It was what he was working on before he disappeared."

"Disappeared?" asked Villa.

"He also built machines for extracting oxygen from the rust," she said, ignoring the question and returning to the original subject. She went over to a rack holding backpacks like the one she had worn. "These are portable units. They're not as effective at producing oxygen as some of the bigger units, but they help. Their filters keep the rust out of your lungs. She took one off the rack and handed it to Villa. He adjusted the straps and put it on.

He reached around behind himself for the mask. "I think I need some help."

She stepped close and helped guide the hose over his shoulder so he could put the mask on. He brushed her fingers as she handed him the mask. She might be strange, but she was not unpleasant to look at.

She frowned and stepped back, her hand on the holstered gun.

Villa held up his hands. "What did I do this time?"

"Rein in your thoughts, Mr. Villa. I have no interest in bedding you. You just as well get that through your head right now."

Villa smiled disarmingly and shrugged. "Why should I? You're an attractive lady who has been here alone ... for quite some time, by all appearances."

"And the sooner I'm alone again, the better."

"Then why don't you go ahead and kill me?" Villa held out his hands.

"Because you can help me with something I *do* want ... and I'm not as cold-blooded as you are."

Villa narrowed his gaze. "All right then, let's see what it is you want from me."

She led the way back upstairs and retrieved her coat, backpack and hat. "It's quite a walk. Do you need some water, or a rest?"

Villa scowled. "One minute you're ready to shoot me. The next, you're nice. Is it any wonder I don't know what to do where you're concerned?"

"You serve no purpose to me passed out," she said, simply.

Pancho Villa blew out a long sigh. "I'd like a little water, please."

She stepped out of the room and returned a moment later with a glass. Villa drank it down, then grimaced. "It's not very good."

"The water here is polluted. It takes a lot of work to get it clean enough to drink."

"All right, I'm ready to go."

She tucked her hair into her hat and strapped the mask over her nose and mouth, grabbed a gray bag and slung it over her shoulder, then led the way outside. "Keep to the shadows," she instructed, "and don't talk unless it's necessary."

"Why is that?"

"Let's just say, I'm not the only person left alive and you're lucky I'm the one who found you."

He followed her in silence through the city toward the southeast. Eventually the buildings began to thin out and they came to an open field. Gray machines in various states of disrepair cluttered the field. Cloth hung in tatters from the wooden frames. What metal was visible was tainted with rust.

The machines were shaped roughly like birds, except that they had two sets of wings instead of one. One set of wings emerged from the roughly cone-shaped body like a bird's. A series of struts held another wing above. A pair of wheels was mounted below the wings. There was a giant wooden fan blade on the wide end of the cone-shaped structure. The pointed end of the cone had three small wing-like structures. Two stuck out to the side, reminding Villa of a bird's tail. One stuck up vertically. There appeared to be two driver's compartments under the wings, just behind the fan-like structure.

"What kind of vehicle is this?" asked Villa. "It looks a little like a bird and a little like a truck."

Alethea shrugged. "I suppose you could think of it that way—a truck of the air."

When she said that, the vehicle made some sense. It must be a flying machine and the fan blade must be an engine, like the ones mounted on airships.

"These machines … they're small compared to airships. How fast are they?"

"Much faster than airships," said Alethea. "And much more maneuverable."

"But more fragile, being made of cloth and wood."

Alethea nodded. "It's those materials that have kept these machines from decaying more than they have."

Villa looked around at all these strange aircraft. He had a

vision of a whole armada flying against a lumbering American airship. It would be like a cavalry charge. "Do these carry gas like an airship? Are they explosive?"

"They carry some fuel for the engines and that can ignite, but it's nowhere near as volatile as the gasses used in airships."

Villa grinned underneath his mask. "With one of these, I could fly to the portal you showed me. I could get home. With a fleet of these, I could drive out the Americans. Can you show me how to fly one?"

"I could, if there was a working one."

Villa's shoulders slumped. "You mean to tell me none of these will actually fly?"

"That's what I need you for." She stepped over to one of the aircraft and patted it on the side. "None of these are in operating condition, but there are so many, I think we could make two of them into working aircraft."

"Why two?"

"One for you to return home," said Alethea. "The other is so I can leave this place and search for my grandfather."

Villa nodded slowly. "I like this plan. I will help you." He held out his hand.

She looked at it suspiciously, then dropped the gray bag to the ground. She opened it and took out a wrench. "There's no better time to start than the present. Take a look around, focus on the engines, and see if you can find parts that aren't too badly rust damaged."

Villa's hand remained suspended in mid-air. "What you ask will require cooperation and trust. Shaking my hand would show that. I promise to be a perfect gentleman while we assemble two aircraft."

She stood slowly. Warily she reached out and shook Villa's hand. He nodded. "See, that wasn't so bad." He let go and started to turn. "I am curious, though. Why don't you speak aloud? I'd be interested to hear your voice."

Alethea spoke strange, gibberish syllables. He had to work to understand the words she thought at the same time. "You wouldn't understand me."

"Is that what I sound like to you?"

Alethea nodded. Again there were gibberish syllables.

"Most likely."

Pancho Villa sighed. With an effort he kept his mouth shut and thought the words, "Then I will endeavor to communicate clearly."

"Perhaps you *can* be a gentleman." Villa sensed that she smiled behind the mask. She pulled out a pocket watch. "Time's wasting. Let's get to work."

# Chapter Six

Maria Reyes wiped down a table in the cantina as the door flew open and Rodolfo Fierro stormed in. Another of Pancho Villa's lieutenants—Guillermo Talamantes—followed close behind. The two men looked terrible. Fierro wore a bandage around his head; blood had seeped through at the temple leaving a brown spot. Talamantes had a visible limp and wore a bandage on his hand. Both were drawn, pale, and unshaven. They sat down and Fierro banged on the table.

"Pulque," growled Fierro when Maria approached.

"Pulque? Not tequila?" asked Maria.

"Tequila is Villa's drink. Besides, pulque is sour like the defeat we just endured." Fierro reached into his pocket and pulled out a pack of rolling papers and a pouch of tobacco.

Maria nodded and went to the bar, listening as the men spoke freely, oblivious to her presence.

"How was it the airships were there?" Talamantes shook his head sadly. The question sounded rhetorical, as though he had asked it many times in the last few days. "Why were all those trucks standing by with barbed wire? How come so many men were awake at such a late hour?"

"They were expecting us." Fierro poured out a little tobacco on one of the rolling papers. "Someone told Pershing our plans." There was a quaver in his voice. Incredulity? Anger? Maria wasn't certain.

"But who? Obregón's men that let us through?"

Fierro shook his head. "They didn't have enough details." He began rolling the paper around the tobacco. "Sure they could have told Pershing we were on our way, but the Americans knew exactly when we planned to strike. They knew things only those of us in command knew."

Maria approached the table discretely and left a bottle of pulque and two glasses. Fierro nodded acknowledgement, dug out a coin and flipped it toward the end of the table. She took the coin and went over to the door, closing it quietly, then continued wiping down the empty tables.

"Then who could it have been?" Talamantes reached for the bottle of pulque and poured two glasses. "Robles? He always seemed a little timid about fighting the Americans."

"Possibly, but Robles was killed. I saw his body myself." Fierro stuck the cigarette in his mouth and lit it.

Talamantes's brow creased. "It could be the plan went wrong."

Fierro inhaled, then blew out a cloud of smoke. "I think we should look at people who went missing."

"The only general missing is Villa."

Fierro placed the cigarette on the edge of the table and drank half the pulque in one swallow.

"No one has been more loyal to the cause of the revolution than Villa," said Talamantes in a harsh whisper.

Maria felt Fierro's gaze fall on her. "Villa changed his name once when he found himself up against the wall with no way out," he said to Talamantes. "He was always friendly with the Americans—movie makers—that writer ... what was his name?"

"Ambrose Bierce," said Talamantes.

Fierro nodded. "Is it so hard to believe that he set up the whole thing? Get himself captured and change his name again? Maybe even disappear up into America where no one would look for him."

Talamantes took another swallow of the pulque, then wiped the milky liquid from his mouth with the back of his sleeve. "I just can't believe it. Villa liked the Americans when they helped our cause, but no one was angrier than him when they crossed the border with their army and airships."

Fierro took another drag on his cigarette and his expression softened. "I want to believe what you say, but where is Villa?"

Talamantes shrugged. "You saw what those airships could do. Maybe he was vaporized. Poof!" He made a flourish with his fingers.

"Maybe you're right." Fierro swallowed another gulp of pulque. "It just bothers me that no one saw what happened." He lifted his cigarette to his lips again. "If it wasn't Villa, we may still have a traitor among us. We may need to consider a quiet retreat instead of another attack."

"Pancho Villa was always a lucky son of a bitch. I bet he'll turn up again. I bet he'll know who betrayed us."

Fierro reached out and put his hand on Talamantes's shoulder. "I hope you're right, my friend." The two stood together and walked out of the cantina.

Maria looked at the clock. There was still an hour before the cantina closed. Over that time, a couple more groups of Villa's men came in, ordered drinks and left. Finally she went to the back and checked in with the owner, who was cleaning dishes. She grabbed a bag, then left, locking the door behind her.

Instead of going to the rooming house, she went to the edge of town, where telegraph poles followed the road. She looked around to make sure that no one was watching, then ducked behind a bush. She exchanged her dress for a pair of pants that were in the bag and slung a coil of wire with a wiretap on one end and a telegraph key at the other. She shimmied up the pole and tapped into the line, then keyed in a message.

A United States Army truck pulled up in front of Álvaro Obregón's headquarters. The general climbed in next to the driver, who took him into the American compound. They passed Pershing's headquarters and continued into the open area around Cerro del Coronel. He saw the cigar-like silver form of the Airship *McKinley* tethered to its mast, swaying gently in the breeze. The truck followed the road to the mountain's summit and stopped by a staircase that ascended into the airship's gondola.

General Obregón climbed the swaying staircase and noted the shiny fork-like structure that hung from a turret below the gondola. When he reached the gondola, a boatswain snapped to attention and piped him aboard. The ship's captain stood with General Pershing by the ship's wheel. Both turned and approached their guest. The captain saluted. "Welcome aboard, sir."

Obregón returned the salute. Pershing reached out and shook his hand. "General, may I introduce Captain Fries?"

"My pleasure," said Obregón, shaking the captain's hand.

"The captain was just briefing me on the performance of the *McKinley's* new weapon," said Pershing. "It—along with the intelligence provided by your people—assured an easy victory over Pancho Villa's forces."

"New weapon? Is that the thing outside that looks like a two-pronged fork?" asked Obregón.

The captain nodded and stepped over to the chart table. On it was a schematic that showed the electrodes and how they were controlled by a gunner in a cabin at the gondola's stern. "The *McKinley* and the *Garfield* have recently been fitted out with plasma projectors. We can essentially fire balls of lightning at any opponent on the ground."

"Yes, I heard about this weapon." Obregón looked toward the ceiling, realizing he stood below a large quantity of hydrogen gas. "Isn't it quite dangerous?"

"We keep it carefully isolated from the hydrogen," said Fries, "and, in many ways it's safer than carrying explosives aboard. The projectors can't fire back at the ship itself and if the generators fail, we simply can't make a plasma ball."

"And there's much less mass than a hold full of ordnance, giving the airships greater maneuverability." General Pershing beamed like a boy proud of a new plaything. After a moment, he turned serious. "I gather you have some news for us."

Obregón nodded. "I am told Pancho Villa has disappeared. His top lieutenants don't know where he went."

Pershing frowned and put his hands behind his back. "He's certainly not among the men we've captured, nor the bodies we recovered." He looked at the captain. "Is it possible you hit him with the plasma cannon?"

Fries nodded. "One of my spotters reported seeing a man who matched Pancho Villa's description. We nearly had him, but he jumped clear. We came back around to the same position. It looked like Villa, but we weren't sure. We fired again and when my spotters swept the area, he was gone."

"So, it's not certain the target was Villa and even if it was, you can't confirm the kill," said Pershing.

Fries swallowed, but nodded. "Yes, sir."

"That's the one problem with these airships, they're so slow, it's hard to double back on a target quickly." Pershing pursed his lips, then looked up at the captain with a heartening smile. "You did well, Captain. I just wish we knew for sure. It might just break the resistance's back."

"Possibly," said Obregón. "His disappearance has fueled speculation that he's a traitor. Others, of course, will be loyal to Villa till the end. If he fails to resurface, it could be just the thing to destroy the morale of his men."

"But if he *does* resurface," interjected Captain Fries, "his legend will grow that much more."

Pershing looked at Obregón. "Have your people keep a close eye out. If Pancho Villa's alive, I want him in custody. It should be much easier now that his army's moved on and he's all alone."

"Then again," said Obregón, "without an army, he can blend in like a chameleon. He has many friends."

"So do we," said Pershing. "I sense the people of Northern Mexico are grateful for the stability and prosperity we've brought."

General Obregón nodded, hoping that was true.

# Chapter Seven

Pancho Villa sat in the forward cockpit of one of the two airplanes he helped Alethea Seton cobble together. The fuselage was a patchwork of cloth, stitched together from several planes. It took parts from nearly a dozen engines to make two that Alethea was convinced would function. Cables to control the ailerons, elevators, and rudder—names he learned from her—came from still more planes. In the process of assembling it all, Villa gained an intimate knowledge of the aircraft along with a fair grasp of the theory of flight.

Sitting in the rear cockpit, she turned the wheel and operated the foot pedals, which were slaved to the ones in Villa's cockpit, explaining what all the operations did. Once she finished her explanation, she had Villa repeat the actions.

"Okay, I think you're ready to get airborne," she said after a few repetitions.

Villa smiled, both at the prospect that he would be going home soon and that he would be able to fly the craft he helped to build. "To do that, we need fuel, right?" He patted the machineguns mounted up front. "It would also be useful if I could find ammunition for these. It will help greatly in my cause when I return home."

Alethea swallowed hard, as though coming to a decision. "I know where we can get fuel. In many ways, I need your help with that even more than actually assembling a functional craft. If there's ammunition left, it will be in the same place."

"All right then," said Villa. "Where do we go?"

"Remember how I told you about being lucky that I was the one who found you?"

Villa nodded.

"We need to find the others."

His brow creased as he thought a question.

"I call them the Morlocks," said Alethea.

"After the monsters in H.G. Wells's *The Time Machine*." Villa nodded.

"I don't know that novel. No doubt your brain is interpreting the word based on what the images from my mind mean to yours. They have taken over basements in the newer part of the city to the northwest. They hoard fuel for their air filtration machines. They don't generate oxygen like my grandfather's machine at the library, but their machines keep out the rust. Every now and then, they surface, looking for food and supplies. They have a handful of guns, including ones they've scavenged from the planes."

Villa pursed his lips. "That explains why some of the machinegun mounts were missing altogether."

Alethea shook her head. "I just wish you hadn't forced me to destroy your gun. I only have the one plasma gun."

Villa reached into his jacket and pulled a gleaming Bowie knife from its concealed sheath. "I've never been unarmed."

For the first time, he read unguarded surprise in her thoughts. There was a brief flash of another thought— "A little more of a gentleman than I knew" —then her mind went quiet. Finally she directed a thought toward him. "That's a little dubious for going up against men armed with guns."

"I only need to sneak up behind one man with a gun, then I'll be the man with the gun."

"All right," she said. "Let's go back to the library, get some dinner and some rest. We'll strike out in the morning."

"Best if we do so before the sun rises." Villa's tone held the confidence of a seasoned commander.

Alethea smirked as she climbed out of the cockpit. "The Morlocks are creatures of the dark. Better if we attack when there's plenty of light outside. It may dissuade them from chasing us."

Villa frowned at the fact that he hadn't thought of that, but then the corner of his mouth twitched upward. "It's your world. You know best."

Pancho Villa awoke with a start the next morning. He felt as though someone had touched him.

"Mr. Villa, it's time to wake up."

He looked around the darkened room for a moment before he remembered the telepathy. He still wasn't used to the fact that Alethea didn't have to be in the same room to speak to him—or to touch him, apparently. His mind began to drift, considering the possibilities.

"Mind your thoughts, Mr. Villa," came a warning voice in his head.

"And mind your manners, Miss Seton. I could do with a little privacy." He felt her chagrin as she withdrew from his mind.

He reached over and opened the shutters, allowing the morning light to stream in. Alethea had given him another room in the library already supplied with a cot and blankets. She never said anything about the room's previous occupant or what became of that person, and he decided not to press.

He dressed quickly and met Alethea out in the main reading room. They had cleared one of the tables and shared their meals there. She had prepared bowls of porridge and was opening a rare can of peaches when he arrived. "We could use the extra energy, and I thought today called for a bit of celebration. If we're successful, you'll make your first flight this afternoon."

"And if we're not successful?" He lifted an eyebrow.

It was another question she didn't answer, but he didn't really require one. According to her, the Morlocks were what were left of the people who operated the machines—the labor class of this world. In his world, he fought for the peasants. Would he be a Morlock in this world? Where would Alethea fit in? She seemed neither a laborer nor an aristocrat. Like most engineers and scientists, she seemed able to walk in both worlds, but fit completely in neither.

They ate in silence, not speaking of the exchange earlier that morning. Once they finished breakfast, they took time to clean up. She checked her plasma gun while Villa donned his field jacket. He strapped the Bowie knife to his belt so he could reach it easily, then hoisted one of the air cycling packs onto his back. He put on a pair of goggles, to keep the rust out of his eyes and then strapped on his pith helmet.

Once they were satisfied they were ready to go, they stepped out into the dim, watery sunlight. As Alethea locked the door, Villa wondered how such tepid light could discourage even a denizen of the darkness. He followed her down the library steps and they proceeded toward the northwestern corner of the city.

As they walked, Villa became increasingly aware of the

sound of machines thrumming from the surrounding buildings and under their feet. Passing a grate, Villa noticed black exhaust spiraling skyward, but thinning and dissipating before it climbed over the tops of the buildings. He concluded the exhaust must contribute to the dismal color of the atmosphere. He looked forward to seeing bright, blue skies again.

Finally, Alethea came to a large, boxy building that looked like a warehouse with two large barn doors in front and a smaller door to the side. She tried the smaller door, but it was locked. Villa stepped in close and pushed his Bowie knife between the door and the wooden frame.

"Stop!" she called.

She pointed to a rocker switch mounted to the door's frame. Reaching up, she held the switch closed while Villa used the knife as a lever. He popped the latch and the door sprang open.

"Find me some wire or something," she said.

He looked around. A roll of twine sat on a workbench near-by. He cut off a length with his knife and handed it to her. She wrapped it around the switch and tied it off. Satisfied it would hold, she continued through the door and grabbed the wooden handle of an electrical contact switch and threw it into position. Lights overhead flared to life and Villa could see the warehouse was filled with machines that appeared to be motorized bicycles of some kind. Several of them were fitted with machineguns salvaged from the airplanes in the field.

Alethea walked along the front row of bikes. One of them had three wheels and a small trailer in back for hauling things. "This will do nicely," she said. "You can drive this one. You won't have to worry about balance." She took a moment and showed him how to start it and how the controls on the han-dlebars worked.

"Okay, let's get to work," she said. With that, she jogged to the back wall, where numerous barrels were stacked next to a set of wooden shelves holding cans. A few feet away stood another set of shelves holding tools. Villa thought he also recognized machinegun belts. She opened one of the cans and sniffed the contents. Satisfied, she handed one to Villa and carried the oth-er herself. Placing them into the small trailer, they went back and retrieved two more. On the way by, Villa retrieved two machinegun belts and slung them over his shoulder. A moment later, Alethea paused with a bemused expression. She set down her fuel can and retrieved a floppy backpack. She did her best to fit it over the air filtration pack, then continued on her way.

Just as they reached the front row of bikes, a voice shouted something in a language Villa didn't recognize. He turned in time to see one of the Morlocks in the doorway. The person—or was it a creature—had pale skin, blotchy with open sores. He wore tattered, gray clothes. His hair was long and greasy. Dark smudges obscured his features. He lifted a gun.

# Chapter Eight

Alethea and Villa dropped to the ground. A moment later, a bullet pounded a crater into the concrete above their heads. She drew her plasma gun and Villa dropped the two ammo belts into the trailer.

"I take it the Morlocks don't know telepathy," he said.

Alethea shook her head.

"Is there a way out of here?"

She pointed her gun toward the two large barn doors. "That's the only way I know."

Villa poked his head up just far enough to see that the Morlock had reached up and was untying the twine wrapped around the alarm switch. He ran forward just as the Morlock finished his task. Before he could raise his gun again, Villa thrust his knife into the creature's belly up to the hilt. The Morlock reached out and locked Villa's neck in a vice-like grip. Although the creature—the man—looked sickly, he was quite strong and Villa couldn't breathe. He thrust his arms upward and dislodged his opponent's hold, then threw a right cross, knocking him back in the wall.

When he turned around, he saw that Alethea had thrown the barn doors open and had taken a seat on one of the bikes. She kicked it into life and looked at him. "Hurry up! They'll be here soon!"

Villa ran to his cycle and climbed on. He tried kick-starting it as Alethea had done but succeeded only in getting an anemic rumble out of the machine. He stood and put his weight into it. This time, the engine roared to life. They rolled out into the street. Morlocks were emerging from the buildings in their path. Many were squinting. Apparently, they did find the light uncomfortable.

Alethea looked over her shoulder and cursed aloud. More Morlocks had emerged from the buildings behind them. "Ride ahead as fast as you can," she said. "I'll catch up."

"What are you going to do?"

"Something stupid!" She aimed her lightning gun inside

the building, where the fuel containers were stored. Villa accelerated full speed toward the Morlocks that blocked his path. There was a whoosh and bright flash from behind. Several of the Morlocks dove out of his way. Others were alarmed by the new turn of events behind him and rushed past, ignoring him altogether. A moment later, Alethea appeared at Villa's side.

"That's not their only supply of vehicles but hopefully I bought us a little time." She surged ahead, leading the way.

Villa chanced a look behind. Two of the Morlocks had rescued bikes from the flames and were gaining. Alethea and Villa turned a corner and he lost sight of their pursuers.

They rode, zigzagging around corners and down backstreets. Finally Alethea stopped and looked around. Villa pulled up beside her. "Where are we heading? The library?"

Alethea shook her head. "No. They'll be waiting there. Let's get to the airfield."

A Morlock walked around a corner down the street. Spotting the fugitives, he yelled something to unseen companions. Although Villa couldn't recognize the words, he guessed it was something along the lines of "There they are!"

Alethea rode forward, then turned down another street. Villa, with his heavier cargo, struggled to keep up with her. They turned a corner and he ducked instinctively as he heard the pop-pop-pop of machinegun fire. Bullets ricocheted off the surrounding bricks. He gritted his teeth as he followed Alethea around another corner and tried to get more speed out of the cycle.

She turned a corner and Villa recognized that they were on the main street, leading out of town. Looking around, he saw the library behind them. Indeed several Morlocks were waiting on the steps. Spotting them, the Morlocks surged toward the street. Fortunately, none of these had vehicles, but a few had guns and began firing.

Alethea darted down another side street and Villa followed. A mile later, the buildings began to thin. Villa caught sight of the abandoned airfield and hope surged that they had escaped. Alethea pulled up beside one of the functional planes and killed her bike's engine. She opened up the plane's fuel tank as Villa pulled up. Before he even climbed off the bike, she reached in and took the first fuel can.  When it was empty, she tossed it aside and grabbed the second.  While she fueled the plane, he slung the ammo belts into the forward cockpit.

As she opened up the third fuel can, Villa looked back toward the city.  Several of the motorized bikes had appeared. "We're out of time," he said.

"Get in the cockpit and activate the switch," she ordered.

He did as she told him and she ran to the front of the plane. The motorbikes raced across the field.

"Contact!" called Villa.

Alethea grabbed hold of the propeller and pulled it down with all her weight.  It spun once, then stopped.  The exhaust pipe that ran alongside the plane's engine coughed out a belch of smoke.

"Open up the throttle and let's try again!" Without waiting for a response, she reached up and pulled on the propeller once more.  This time, it spun to life.  Villa let go of the switch, then grabbed hold of the brake.  The motorbike riders opened fire just as Alethea climbed into the rear cockpit.  Villa released the brake and let Alethea take control.  She accelerated down the open field, away from the motorbikes.

"Hold onto the controls lightly, so you can follow along with what I'm doing," she called over the loud rumbling of the engine.  She pulled back on the wheel and the plane began to rise into the sky.  There was a hollow feeling in the pit of Villa's stomach as they climbed out of firing range.  A moment later, they swerved around, just over the bikers' heads.

Villa looked at the altimeter, then looked at the buildings ahead.  "We're not getting much lift!"

"We won't," she said.  "The air's too thin.  But we'll get enough."

Gradually, the plane began to gain altitude.  They just cleared the first couple of rooftops.  A marksman appeared on top of one of the buildings and began firing at them.

"Okay, you've got the controls," said Alethea.

"What?  Why now?"

"There's no time like the present."

Villa grabbed the wheel and turned it, adjusting the ailerons while using his feet to control the rudder pedals.  The plane turned onto its side, banking hard. He quickly turned it back before they went into a roll. Finally, he straightened out the plane's course.

"Very good," said Alethea. "You're getting the hang of it. Steer a course toward the portal. You'll need to gain some more altitude."

He did as she told him, glad to be getting away from the Morlocks and looking forward to returning to his own world. He finally caught sight of the strange blue hole in the sky and saw they were a little low. He pulled back on the wheel and the plane climbed.

"You're an excellent student," said Alethea. "Do you think you can land this thing before it runs out of fuel?"

"With your help, I'm sure I can," said Villa with a big grin.

"I'm afraid you won't have it."

He turned around and looked at her. She was unbuckling her harness.

"What the hell are you doing? Come with me! My world is better than this one!"

"Your world's in the middle of a war, Mr. Villa. You don't belong in my world and I don't belong in yours. Win your revolution. Free your people." She climbed out of the seat and dropped from the plane.

Pancho Villa yelled after her. A moment later, the backpack she grabbed at the warehouse opened up and a great white sheet unfurled, slowing her descent. He looked ahead and saw he was approaching the portal. He thought about diving below it, turning around and landing again. Gritting his teeth, he realized she was right. She had survived this long and he needed to get back to his people. A single tear pooled in the bottom of his goggles as he accelerated toward the portal.

# Chapter Nine

When Pancho Villa reached the hole, he nearly lost control of the airplane. Swept into an unseen maelstrom, the wings and fuselage rattled and groaned. The wheel threatened to rip itself from his hands. His knuckles whitened as he fought to keep the plane on a straight course. Finally, he emerged into a calm, blue sky. Looking over the side, he discovered he was much higher than expected and the terrain was unfamiliar.

He pushed the wheel forward, sending the plane into a slow descent. He flew over reddish brown desert cut through by washes. He checked the compass and got his bearings. There were mountains to the northwest and a small town to the east. The land beyond the town rose again. Another range of mountains stood to the south. He turned toward the town and continued his descent. Finally, he spotted a road. That would give him a level place to land. Less than a mile from town was a swath of green that appeared to be a wash or a creek.

Villa checked his fuel gauge. He could remain airborne for another thirty minutes, but scanning the area again, he didn't think he would find a better place to land in that time. He brought the plane down slowly and throttled back as Alethea had instructed him. As the descent continued, it felt as though the ground rushed up to meet him. He throttled back more, but the engine sputtered. Realizing that wasn't a good idea, he gave it more power.

All too soon, the wheels hit the dirt road, sending up a spray of dust and debris. The plane bounced, then came down again. He throttled back until the engine choked and the propeller slowed. The plane rattled along the road, bucking harder than it had on the journey through the hole. He reached down and grabbed the brake. The wheels locked and the plane spun off the road, through a patch of mesquite and finally stopped when it bumped into a tree at the edge of the river.

Villa fell back and breathed a sigh of relief. He lifted the goggles and climbed out of the cockpit. The rocks in the road and the scraggly mesquite branches had torn the plane's fuselage and wings. It sat against a stand of trees, looking little better than it had a few days before. He walked back to the road and looked at the holes and troughs gouged by the plane's wheels when they hit. Although the plane was visible from the road, he realized most people seeing it wouldn't recognize it as anything other than an abandoned machine.

Returning to the stand of trees, he broke off several branches and tossed them over the wings and tail. He returned to the road and looked again. As he hoped, it gave the impression of a machine abandoned a long time ago and a casual observer would take little interest. With some help he could hide it better. He wiped his hands and set out for the town, which he guessed was no more than two miles away.

As he reached the outskirts, he saw an imposing, blocky building. On top were red letters that spelled out "Hotel Gadsden."

"Holy Mother of God," he exclaimed. "I'm in America!" He had stayed at Douglas, Arizona's Gadsden Hotel once and even dined in its lounge with General Pershing before the invasion. A slow grin lifted his mustache. Several loyal followers lived just across the border in Agua Prieta. They could help him hide the plane. What's more, Douglas was on the El Paso and Southwestern Railroad's route. The best inventor he knew could be there in a matter of days.

Rodolfo Fierro groomed his horse and considered the situation. The Americans had resumed their blockade of Madera. Not only were Fierro and his men nearly out of money and supplies, the town's citizens were beginning to feel the pressure as well. There was growing talk of simply turning the revolutionaries over to the Americans so they would end the blockade. In fact, several of his men had already deserted. He gathered some of those men had taken advantage of the weak point at Buenaventura to escape the area and return home. Others had turned themselves in at Cuauhtémoc, where it was rumored the Americans would grant amnesty if the revolutionaries disarmed. At one time, Rodolfo Fierro would have been angry about the desertions.

Now he hardly blamed them.

Villa would have persuaded the men and the villagers to stick with the revolution. Fierro lacked Villa's charisma or political savvy. He could lead men in battle, but he didn't know how to battle empty stomachs, especially when he harbored his own doubts about the cause. After all, he fought so farmers and laborers could have the same rights as the aristocracy. Wasn't that what the American's offered? Wasn't that why Obregón joined them?

Fierro would lead the men away soon—probably through the mountains and into Sonora as he and Villa had once considered. Once there, they could join forces with revolutionaries in Hermosillo or Nogales and consider a sensible course of action.

A boy cleared his throat. "Excuse me," he said. "Are you Mr. Fierro?"

Fierro turned and nodded.

"A telegram just arrived for you."

"For me?" Fierro's eyebrows came together. "Who's it from?"

"I don't know. It came from Agua Prieta and it's signed D.A."

Fierro shook his head, even more confused, but took the paper and dug out a precious one-centavo coin to tip the boy. The telegram read, "Taken out of action at Chihuahua. Found my way back. Meet me in Agua Prieta. D.A."

"D.A.," said Fierro aloud. "Doroteo Arámbula?" His eyes went wide. Could it be that Pancho Villa had resurfaced? If so, he needed to find out where Villa had been, and more importantly, what he planned next. He finished grooming his horse, then saddled and bridled her. A few minutes later, he rode forth.

As he expected, Pancho Villa found several men loyal to the revolution in Agua Prieta. Although there was an American military presence along the border with men stationed at Fort Huachuca, Camp San Bernardino and Camp Douglas, actual patrols of the border were sparse. In three days, Villa saw two sets of mounted soldiers ride through the area and once from his room in the Hotel Gadsden he saw an American airship glide along the border. He reasoned the Americans weren't expecting anyone to bring the battle to them.

The sparse patrols allowed a few men at a time to follow the Rio Agua Prieta to the airplane. Villa instructed them to make a hiding place for the flying machine among the short trees. Once finished, it was still visible from the road but much less conspicuous—as though it were just a discarded piece of farm equipment.

Four days after returning from the mysterious world of rust, Villa met the train. A white-haired man wearing the peaked cap of a ship captain, a blue waistcoat and no jacket emerged from the coach. Villa stepped forward and extended his hand. "Captain Cisneros, it's been a long time."

"A pleasure to see you again, Francisco," Cisneros replied. As a young man, Onofre Cisneros attended university and became a mining engineer during the French occupation of Mexico. After the revolution, he moved to Ensenada, where he built machines for underwater construction and exploration. He hoped to develop the port into one that could rival those at Los Angeles and San Francisco to the north. President Porfirio Diaz attempted to take control of the port and seize his inventions. Cisneros opposed the government ever since, supporting the revolution.

Cisneros and Villa rode out to the place where the airplane was concealed. Villa uncovered the plane and Cisneros stood back with his hands on his hips. "Well I'll be damned—a practical heavier than air flying machine, and she's a beauty, too." He stepped up and ran his hands along the wings as though he caressed a lover.

He looked at the scratches and tears in the plane's skin. "She's seen some rough treatment, but nothing we can't put right again."

"What I want to know is, can you make more of them?"

"Well, I can certainly draw up plans. If we can find a workshop, we should be able to make parts. Nothing here looks too difficult." Cisneros examined the engine. "Internal combustion engine, similar to the ones on trucks and airships, very nice. Where's the fuel tank?"

Villa led him around to the far side of the plane and opened a cap near the engine compartment. Cisneros sniffed, then stuck his finger in the tube and rubbed his fingers together.

"Whatever this thing runs on, it's not conventional gasoline," stated the engineer.

Villa's brow knitted. "What do you mean?"

"It smells different than gasoline and much stronger. It evaporates off my fingers and leaves no residual odor." Cisneros shrugged. "Interesting stuff. Where did you get it?"

Villa shook his head. "It doesn't really matter. I can't get more. The question is, will it run on regular gasoline?"

Cisneros pushed open the engine housing. "I think so. At most, some of the fittings and valves may need adjustment or replacement, but I think we could have it ready in a few days."

"Excellent," said Villa. "Just let me know what you need to get started."

# Chapter Ten

Maria Reyes left her rooming house and walked down Madera's main street to the cantina. Over the past few days, the streets had grown strangely quiet. Revolutionaries were leaving town. She knew there had been desertions, but when she saw Rodolfo Fierro ride out of town a few days ago she knew something else was going on. He might not always agree with Pancho Villa, but he would not simply abandon the cause of revolution.

Arriving at the cantina, she saw Guillermo Talamantes sitting alone, finishing lunch. She sat down next to him. "Mr. Talamantes, sir, a lot fewer of the men have been coming into the cantina. I've heard many have left town. Has the … is the revolution over? Have we lost?" She wrung her hands nervously.

Talamantes shook his head while he scooped up a few beans with his tortilla. "Nothing like that." He paused and took a bite, then continued to speak even as he chewed. "Oh sure, there have been some cowardly dogs and you can be sure if I ever see them, I'll shoot them between the eyes myself." He swallowed the food and followed it with a gulp of beer, then leaned forward conspiratorially. "Pancho Villa is alive."

"Alive!" Maria gasped and sat up straight.

He held his finger to his lips. "You mustn't tell anyone. I've been sworn to secrecy, but we're sending the men north, little by little, to Agua Prieta. Villa, he has a surprise for the gringos."

"Oh thank you, Mr. Talamantes. I've been so worried about my Doroteo. I miss him so."

He took another bite and leered at her as he chewed. "Yes, he was very fond of you."

She stood, but hesitated. "I don't suppose there's a way I could go to Agua Prieta."

Talamantes looked around, apparently afraid of being overheard even though there was no one else in the cantina. He motioned her back to the chair, then shook his head. "It'll be very dangerous."

"I want to help the cause. I can cook. I can mend clothes. I can be a nurse. Please, let me have a chance to prove myself.

I would do anything for Doroteo … for the revolution."

He popped the remainder of the tortilla into his mouth, then sat back and chewed thoughtfully. "The supplies we have left fit in a couple of wagons. I'm sending one north tomorrow." Talamantes swallowed. "They're sure to be inspected in Buenaventura. It's just possible that an attractive woman could … distract Obregón's men."

Maria made an effort to look shocked. A moment later, she brought it under control. Finally, she nodded as though reaching a decision. "I'm committed to the revolution, Mr. Talamantes. If that would help the cause and bring me closer to my Doroteo, I'll do it."

"Very well. Meet me at Apodaca's Livery tomorrow at sunrise."

"Thank you, Mr. Talamantes. You won't regret this." She smiled, then stood and went to the kitchen to retrieve her apron and a towel. Once there, she took a moment, to close her eyes and attempt to shut out the memories of a sound like an over-ripe melon smashed into a wall. After work, she would send a message to her employer, letting him know she was leaving Madera to follow a lead on the whereabouts of Pancho Villa.

Rodolfo Fierro rode from Agua Prieta, Sonora into Douglas, Arizona without meeting a soldier or a lawman. The United States Army didn't care if one man or even a small party crossed the border. The Americans believed the Mexican Army had been driven south of Zacatecas and Pershing had contained the revolutionaries. Airships patrolling the border would see a large force before they were close enough to be a problem.

Fierro saw the tall red letters proclaiming "Hotel Gadsden" from the edge of town. He wound his way through the streets of Douglas and tied his horse to a hitching post out front. Stepping through the doors, his mouth fell open as he caught sight of the polished wooden pillars supporting the roof and the grand marble staircase leading upstairs. A Tiffany stained glass mural adorned the wall at the top of the stairs.

He collected himself and walked over to a couch upholstered

in supple leather. He took out his tobacco pouch and some rolling papers, then sat. As he rolled a cigarette, Pancho Villa and an old man appeared at the top of the staircase. They walked down, speaking quietly to each other. Villa smiled broadly when he reached the bottom. "Rodolfo!" he called. "You made it!"

"I wonder how many men we could feed with the price of one night's lodging in this palatial hotel," snarled Fierro.

Villa nodded. "The Hotel Gadsden is not very expensive, my friend—cheaper than the rooming houses of Agua Prieta and I'm easily recognized there."

Fierro lit his cigarette and snorted, sending a burst of smoke from his nostrils. "Many wondered if you had deserted like our friend Álvaro Obregón."

Villa led the way to the door. "Is this really the welcome I get from an old friend?"

"Where have you been all this time?" asked Fierro.

"That will take a while to explain," said Villa. "What's more important is what I brought with me."

Outside, Fierro retrieved his horse and followed Villa to a livery stable down the street. Along the way, Villa introduced Onofre Cisneros. They hitched two horses to a small flatbed wagon that held a toolbox, an assortment of machine parts and several five-gallon cans. They rode a short distance out of town to the Rio Agua Prieta. There, concealed among the trees, was a machine shaped roughly like a bird with two sets of wings. Most of the machine's body looked as though it were covered in a gray patchwork quilt, but the tail held vivid red, white and green stripes—the colors of Mexico.

"You mean to tell me that you fell down some kind of hole into a different world and that's where you found this ... what is it?" Fierro scratched his head.

"It's called an airplane." Villa puffed out his chest. "They're fast, not like the lumbering airships. We can build an airborne cavalry, where we'll never be tripped up by barbed wire."

"I'll have to see it to believe it," said Fierro.

Together, they pushed the machine out into the open. Cisneros attached a spout to one of the five-gallon cans, then poured the contents into a receptacle near the machine's engine. Villa climbed into a seat between the two wings and Cisneros went up front and grabbed something that looked like a giant wooden fan blade. Villa yelled "Contact" and Cisneros pulled down as hard as he could.

The fan blade spun to life with a roar and the two men cheered. Fierro scowled at the fierce noise, not willing to be impressed until he saw the machine fly. He turned away and looked off into the distance. He tossed his cigarette aside as he caught sight of a silvery glint, then swung around.

"American airship!" he shouted.

Villa cupped his hand to his ear. "What?"

Fierro pointed and Villa dropped into the seat with a curse. A moment later, the noise stopped and the fan blade slowed.

"Quick," called Villa. "We've got to push the plane back into its hiding place." He climbed out of the seat and all together they pushed the plane back into its shelter among the trees.

Looking up through the branches, Fierro saw the airship pass overhead.

It took slightly less than a week for the supply wagon to travel from Madera to Agua Prieta. They had no problem passing the blockade at Buenaventura. The supply wagon's driver handed a stack of pesos to one of Obregón's men and they were soon on their way. By the time they arrived, Maria Reyes was stiff and sore from long days sitting on a buckboard and nights sleeping on the ground.

After two months in the quiet mountain village of Madera, Maria found the dusty border town depressing. There were few trees and the squat, adobe buildings seemed dismal to her. The American town of Douglas across the border seemed little better. A curtain of gauze-like cirrus clouds covered the sky adding to her sense of gloom. She missed Zacatecas and was ready for this mission to be over. She only hoped she had picked the side that really would bring peace and prosperity to a troubled land.

A sound that was part roar and part high-pitched growl broke through her melancholy. She looked skyward and saw something that looked like a mechanical bird. Her first thought was that she was seeing some new American invention. Then she noticed the colors of the Mexican flag on the tail and wing.

A few steps up the street, she saw one of Villa's men who had left Madera ahead of her. She walked up to him and pointed. "What in the world is that?"

"Pancho Villa is teaching Rodolfo Fierro to fly," said the young man whose name she couldn't remember.

"What?"

"Ay, General Villa says he's going to build a cavalry of the air. We'll be able to fight those gringo airships on their own terms."

The bird-like machine made a long sweeping turn and sped through the sky faster than any vehicle she had ever seen. Her gaze narrowed as it passed overhead. All at once the dusty border town of Agua Prieta held much more promise than she expected. It was time to find out where Pancho Villa had disappeared to and where he was building his cavalry of the air.

# Chapter Eleven

Pancho Villa sat across from Maria Reyes in the restaurant at the Hotel Gadsden. She had risked bandits, Americans and turncoat Mexicans to be with him. She probably felt safe among his men, feeling they would protect her or risk their leader's wrath. As he sipped a glass of wine, he wondered if such faith was misplaced.

Villa had no problem going through a wedding ceremony to appease a pretty woman—someone to distract him from the rigors of warfare—but he had only one wife and she was safe in the south. None of those women had traveled across country to be by his side. None of those women had seemed to give more than lip service to the revolution. Maria said she wanted to help. Villa couldn't help but admire such a woman and her spirit aroused him.

"Tell me about the world of rust," said Maria.

Villa described the strange land of decaying buildings and machines. He described fighting the Morlocks, but he avoided mentioning Alethea. Even as he spoke, he wondered what became of her. Why had she jumped? Were the Morlocks waiting for her? If she got away, was she searching for her grandfather?

Maria's bravery was palpable, but it paled compared to Alethea's. Still, Villa found he respected Maria a great deal. Such respect required honesty. He reached out and took her hand. "Maria, you took many risks for me, traveling to the border." He shook his head as he struggled for words. "The world of rust ... changed me. I need to focus on the cause of the revolution, not on a ... relationship."

Her face crumpled and she looked down at her plate as though she was going to cry, but to her credit no tears actually flowed. She was strong and Villa admired her even more. He wondered if he was making a mistake, sending her away. He stood and took her hands, then pulled her close. She was trembling, but that subsided as she melted into him. "I will love you and the revolution, no matter what, Doroteo."

Villa's thoughts and emotions were a vortex, like the one to the world of rust. He was tempted to snatch back his words and keep Maria by his side, but Alethea's face haunted him as did the face of his wife. He needed some fresh air and he needed to change the subject. "Would you like to see the workshop where we're building the air cavalry?"

She sniffed, then nodded.

Villa left a coin on the table and they departed the hotel. As they walked through the door, Rodolfo Fierro stepped up, a cigarette dangling from his mouth. His gaze narrowed when he saw Maria. "Our waitress from Madera. What a surprise."

"I just arrived in town," said Maria.

"Guillermo Talamantes arranged for her to travel with the supply wagon," interjected Villa. "It was very brave of her to make the journey."

"Indeed." Fierro nodded slowly. "These are dangerous times for a woman alone."

"We all must endure danger if the revolution is to succeed," she said.

Fierro took a drag on the cigarette and blew smoke out through his nose. Without another word, he continued on. Villa led Maria down the street, feeling as though Fierro's gaze lingered on his back.

They walked a few streets until they came to a large, brick building. It struck Villa how much it looked like the buildings in the world of rust. He opened the wooden door. Inside were lathes and drill presses. Scrap metal lay against a wall. Lumber had been stacked against another wall.

"I thought people would be hard at work on a second airplane," said Maria.

"They will be, soon enough," said Villa. "We need more supplies, but we're almost out of money."

She looked at him wide eyed.

"Don't worry, we're not far from Fort Huachuca and they have everything we need."

There was a knock at General John J. Pershing's door. A moment later, Major Burton looked in. "The photographs have been developed, sir."

"Thank you." Pershing stood and straightened his jacket, then crossed to the door. A lieutenant was laying out a set of photographs along the dining room table.

"These were taken just outside of Douglas, Arizona," explained Burton as the general took out a set of glasses and set them on his nose.

Pershing peered at the photos. They showed a stand of trees near a riverbed. Concealed among the trees was some kind of machine. Three men were visible in one of the photos. Pershing picked up a magnifying glass and examined first one photo then the other. "I'll be damned if that isn't Pancho Villa and Rodolfo Fierro."

"The intelligence boys agree, sir," said Burton.

Pershing stood up straight and removed his glasses. "This was definitely taken over United States territory?"

"The *Lincoln* had just taken her bearings. Douglas was due east of their position." Major Burton frowned. "There's no question, Pancho Villa has invaded the United States."

Pershing pointed at the photos with his glasses. "What do you make of this machine they're with?"

"It's well hidden in the trees and they've clearly tossed branches over parts of it." Burton grabbed a roll of vellum and rolled it over one of the photos. It showed an outline that looked a little like a bird with outstretched wings. "This is the thing's overall shape."

"What has he got? Some kind of flying machine?" The general's brow knitted.

A captain stepped up, cleared his throat and saluted. "General Obregón to see you, sir."

The Mexican general stood in the doorway. Pershing beckoned him over. "What do you make of this?"

Obregón pursed his lips as he studied the photographs. He nodded and stood up. "I didn't believe it when I first heard it, but now I wonder."

"Believe what?" asked Pershing.

"My spy who is watching Villa says he's developed some kind of aircraft. Much faster than an airship and armed with machine guns."

Major Burton narrowed his gaze. "That's incredible. Does it actually fly?"

Obregón nodded. "It does, but he only has one. So far."

Both Pershing and Burton looked at Obregón. "What do you mean?" asked Pershing.

"He intends to raid Fort Huachuca to get the parts he needs to build more," said Obregón.

Burton smacked his fist in his palm. "By God, we'll be ready for him, just like we were in Chihuahua."

"We'll do more than be ready for him. My old command is stationed at Huachuca. We'll flush that bird right out of the trees." Black Jack Pershing grinned. "Pancho Villa has just fucked with the wrong man."

Maria Reyes was on her way to the Hotel Gadsden to get some dinner and call it a night, when a voice cried out behind her to open the door. She turned and saw Pancho Villa riding full tilt. She grabbed the door, opened it, and Villa rode straight into the lobby. She rushed through behind him and watched wide-eyed as he continued up the steps toward the Tiffany glass at the mezzanine. The horse's shoe chipped off a piece of marble on the seventh step. The man behind the desk shouted, but Villa drew his pistol and fired four shots, then called for Cisneros and Fierro. The man behind the desk ducked down, out of sight.

Cisneros emerged from behind a dark, wooden door that opened onto the mezzanine. Fierro appeared below at the door that led into the adjoining saloon. "What's going on, Jefe?" called Fierro.

"Black Jack Pershing's Buffalo Soldiers are marching this way from Fort Huachuca. They'll be here by morning." He rode the rest of the way up to the mezzanine and looked down at Cisneros. "Come with me. We've got to get the plane ready." He helped the old man up to the back of his horse, then rode the animal down the stairs. It was much more skittish going down the marble steps than climbing them. Villa pointed his gun toward Fierro. "Roust the men. Get them marching up the

Bisbee road. We've got to cut them off before they pin us down."

Fierro darted back into the saloon as Villa reached the lobby floor. He looked down at Maria, as though noticing her for the first time. "Make sure the infirmary is ready. We're sure to have a lot of wounded men this time tomorrow."

She nodded hurriedly. "I'll go there right now."

He gathered up the reins and made as though to snap them, but was interrupted by Maria's voice. "Doroteo, be careful."

He slid effortlessly out of the saddle and swept Maria into his arms, nearly crushing her. His kiss was more violent than tender. They parted breathless. "I'll see you soon," he said. He gathered the horse's reins and led it through the lobby and out the door.

As she turned to leave, she became aware of Fierro standing in the saloon's door, his gaze fixed firmly upon her. He tipped his hat, then brushed past her and out into the street.

Maria whirled around and hurried to the workshop where they were collecting parts for more airplanes. She let herself in. One corner of the room was stocked with medical supplies. She lit a kerosene lamp and took her time checking everything over, then waited until well after nightfall. At that point, she blew out the lamp and allowed her eyes to adjust to the darkness.

She crept to a locked door—the office belonged to the inventor, Onofre Cisneros. Reaching into her blouse, she retrieved a concealed pouch and took out a lock pick. A moment later, she had the door open. The inner office was even darker, but she knew right where the plans were. She went to the desk and rolled up the papers.

A light fell across her. Startled, she brought the roll of papers to her chest.

A figure was silhouetted in the doorway. He held a kerosene lantern in one hand and wielded a knife in the other. "What the hell are you doing?" growled Rodolfo Fierro.

"You must think I'm the spy for General Pershing." She shook her head and took a step back.

He barked out a laugh. "You? Spying for Pershing? Of course not."

She narrowed her gaze. "You mean you don't suspect me?"

"Oh, you're clearly spying for someone, but it's not Pershing."

"How do you know that?"

"Because *I'm* spying for Pershing."

"You? Why?" Maria's eyes widened.

"I don't like Pershing in our country, but too many of our men are going hungry. Villa is dangerous and reckless. He needs to be stopped." Fierro took a step forward.

"What? So you can take command?"

"So I can lead the revolutionaries south and present a unified force to drive the Americans out."

"Then what? Go back to fighting among yourselves like dogs." Maria snorted. "Two years ago, my mother was raped and murdered by Venustiano Carranza's men. Six months later, Pancho Villa bashed my papa's head in with a lead pipe. I only survived because my papa hid me in the cellar before the men stormed the house—but I heard. I heard everything." A single tear fell, but she made no move to wipe it away. "Mexico has been tearing itself apart for years. If my employers can keep us from committing suicide without subjugating us, then I welcome it, Mr. Fierro. I welcome it."

Fierro stepped into the room and she could see his teeth barred. "Just who are your 'benevolent' employers, Miss Reyes? It's bad enough the United States wants to make us part of its empire. Who else has eyes on poor undeveloped México?"

Her hand slipped into her blouse and came out with a derringer. He smiled at the sight of the gun and lunged forward. She put a bullet right between his eyes. Rodolfo Fierro dropped to his knees, then fell face down onto the office floor. Stepping carefully around him, she disappeared into the night.

# Chapter Twelve

Pancho Villa dropped Cisneros by the livery stable so he could hitch up the wagon containing tools and gasoline for the airplane. He then rode across the border to Agua Prieta and summoned a half dozen loyal men to help him get the plane ready for the next day's battle. Within the hour, they were on the Bisbee road, riding to the plane's hiding place in the channel of the Rio Agua Prieta. A mile out of town, they caught up with Onofre Cisneros and his wagon, slowly trudging along the road.

"I thought you would have been there already, my friend," said Villa.

Cisneros grinned. "You have a limited amount of ammunition for your guns. I had an idea for a weapon that could wreak havoc with the American soldiers." He pointed over his shoulder to a case of bottles. "I can mix together some oil and gasoline, then add in an alcohol-dipped fuse and we can drop it on the American soldiers from above."

Villa smiled broadly. "I like it! It's like a cocktail mixed especially for Black Jack Pershing's men."

"A very incendiary cocktail," agreed Cisneros.

They reached the plane's hiding place and Cisneros directed the men to push the aircraft out of the wash and up onto the level ground beside the road. He checked the oil and the fuel levels, then set to work mixing the leftover oil and fuel into the bottles he brought. Villa assigned guard rotations, then retrieved some beef jerky and tortillas from his saddlebags for a light supper while one of the men made a campfire and began cooking a pot of beans.

As the men ate their supper, Villa retrieved a bedroll from the back of his horse, who was contentedly grazing from the tall grass of the riverbed. He lay his bedroll down next to the plane and looked up at the deepening sky. The hole to the world of rust hovered high overhead and Villa found himself wondering what Alethea was doing. Perhaps after this battle—after more airplanes were built—Villa would fly back through the hole and see what was happening in that strange, alternate Chihuahua.

As the first stars appeared in the sky, Villa fell into a sound sleep. He awoke just a few hours later to the sound of men singing to the rhythm of hoof beats. He opened one eye and saw his men riding along the Bisbee road to confront the Buffalo Soldiers. Guillermo Talamantes rode in front, but he didn't catch sight of Rodolfo Fierro—not really surprising given the darkness and the way the men were grouped.

Villa climbed from his bedroll, grabbing two pistols which lay beside him. He leapt to his feet and fired the pistols into the air. "Viva la revolución! Viva México!"

The men shouted back in response and several shots were fired into the air. Heartened by their fierce loyalty, Villa donned two bandoliers. The guard on duty stirred the campfire back into life and started a fresh pot of coffee. The remaining guards were roused by the gunfire. Cisneros climbed out of his bedroll, put on his boots and disappeared into the tall brush to relieve himself.

Villa handed him a cup of coffee when he returned. He drank it with a grimace. Once they were a little more awake, they transferred the improvised bombs into the rear seat of the airplane. Sunlight colored the sky and Villa could see his cavalrymen come to a halt and begin forming up ranks. Apparently the enemy was in sight.

Villa donned his pith helmet and climbed into the forward cockpit. Cisneros climbed in behind him, while one of the soldiers took position at the front of the plane. "Contact!" he called.

The soldier pulled down on the propeller and it sputtered into motion. Villa released the brake and taxied the plane out onto the road. He opened up the throttle and felt the wind blow past him. He nearly reached his own soldiers when the plane lifted into the air. As he gained altitude, he heard the first shots fired.

He made a circle over the battlefield, getting a sense of how the ranks were formed. He loved this vantage point and wished he had some way of communicating with the officers on the ground.

A group of American infantrymen broke off and marched around the revolutionary flank. Villa turned the plane and pointed downward. Cisneros lit one of the incendiary bombs and dropped it over the side. A moment later, there was a loud whoosh and a fireball erupted in the midst of the American soldiers. Some fell dead and the rest scattered.

Villa lifted the plane into an arc, then swung around into a dive. He could see the American soldiers on the ground in front of him. He shouted for Cisneros to take the controls as he grabbed the machineguns and began firing. He laughed as he saw men drop their weapons and scatter. Before they got too low, Cisneros lifted the plane. This time, shots from the ground trailed them as they gained altitude. One ripped through the outer edge of the starboard wing.

While Cisneros manned the controls, Villa took time to get a better look at the battlefield. Just as he thought he had spotted his next target, he saw a glint on the horizon. He looked up and spat a curse. An American airship was approaching from the east. "We can't let them join the battle!" called Villa.

"What can we do against the airship?" shouted Cisneros.

Villa patted the machineguns. "It's a big gas bag. We'll punch some holes in it!"

Cisneros shook his head. "It's not just one gas bag. It's lot of gas bags in a steel frame. You'd have to punch holes in a lot of them to do any good. Better to direct your fire at the tail, knock out her steering if you can."

Villa nodded. "Take the controls!"

Cisneros accelerated toward the airship while Villa took careful aim with the machineguns. He fired at the rudder as they made their first pass. Several holes appeared in the tail, but the rudder moved slightly, as though it was still being controlled from the gondola. Villa shook his head, not convinced they had accomplished anything.

As they flew away, Villa kept his eyes on the airship. The crew had deployed the lightning gun and the electrodes glowed blue. "We need to do something quickly, or they're going to decimate our men!"

"Take the controls," shouted Cisneros. "Get in close, over the tail, I have an idea."

Villa banked, turning the plane back toward the airship. Cisneros lit one of the incendiary cocktails. As they swept past, he dropped the bottle onto the airship's aileron fin. It bounced and rolled toward the rear. As it reached the back of the tail, it erupted in a ball of flame. The airship listed onto its side and Villa sped forward. Looking down, he saw a ball of spinning lightning on the electrodes. It leapt from the airship as the flames from the tail worked their way forward, engulfing and blackening the dirigible.

A moment later, the airplane was rocked by a tremendous force. Villa felt the rudder pedals give way. Looking back, he saw that their tail was a smoking ruin. Although he still had altitude control, he only had slight control of the airplane's direction through its elevators and ailerons. If he could find level enough ground, he could land the airplane, but by the time he got down, the battle would be over.

He looked back and saw with satisfaction that the airship was in worse shape than the plane. The structure was almost entirely engulfed in flame and smoke as it sank tail-first toward the ground. Men jumped from the gondola. Grimly, Villa thought they were too high and it was unlikely many of them would survive. At least he had saved his men from the lightning gun. He turned his attention back to the problem of where to land.

Looking ahead, he saw that they were flying in the general direction of the gaping blood-red hole in the sky. Gritting his teeth, Villa lifted the plane and hoped he would reach the place where he could find parts for repair. He had been through the tunnel and come back once before. He was certain he could do it again.

General Pershing frowned as he leafed through the report of Pancho Villa's raid on Douglas, Arizona. His former regiment from Fort Huachuca had done a fantastic job. They had rounded up most of the Villistas and captured the building where Villa was building his aircraft. Inside, one of Villa's top aids, Rodolfo Fierro had been found dead, a bullet in his brain. However, the plans for the aircraft were gone. What's more, although several men on the battlefield reported seeing Villa's aircraft hit by the *Lincoln's* final shot, his men could find no wreckage nor could they find the bodies of Pancho Villa or his co-pilot. It's possible the craft was simply vaporized. Part of him hoped so. Part of him knew that he hadn't seen the last of heavier than air craft that could fly circles around airships.

"Do you think this is the end of the revolution?" asked Major Burton.

Pershing stood up and went to the window. He put his hands behind his back and looked out at the newly completed wall. "Hard to say. We won a major victory, but we lost one of our airships—one of our most powerful weapons. Will Villa be a martyr and inspire others? Will he turn up somewhere else?" He shook his head. "We won a victory, but it's not as clear cut as I would have liked."

"Are victories every as clear as we'd like, sir?" asked Burton.

Pershing took a deep breath and let it out slowly. "No, I suppose they rarely are." He crossed to a hutch at the other end of the room and took out two glasses and a decanter of scotch. He poured a glass and handed it to Burton, then poured a glass for himself. "To the men of the *Lincoln*," he said.

"Here, here." Burton tossed back his drink, then set the glass on the table.

Pershing sipped his scotch, then stared into the golden liquid. "I just wish I knew what happened to the plans for that aircraft Villa was flying."

# Afterword:
## The Road to Rust and Ruin

Thank you for reading *Revolution of Air and Rust* and I truly hope you have enjoyed it. The road to this story started more years ago than I care to think about. I credit *Star Trek* with introducing me to many fine science fiction writers. I discovered several of my favorite authors—people like Jerome Bixby, David Gerrold, and Harlan Ellison—by seeing their names attached to *Star Trek* episodes. Shortly after the first *Star Trek* movie, when Pocket Books began publishing novels in the franchise, I added several other favorites to my list. One of those was Robert E. Vardeman.

Those favorite authors instilled in me a love of storytelling. I've been interested in writing as long as I can remember. Not only did I want to write science fiction, I imagined writing westerns, horror stories, fantasy and more. Somewhere along the line, my parents convinced me that I should, at least, have a backup career that would earn some money if this writing thing didn't work out. So, I started on a path toward becoming an astronomer as well. So much for making money....

Anyway, one summer while I was in college, I took a job at a place called Maria Mitchell Observatory located on Nantucket Island in Massachusetts. At the time I was there, research was conducted on a Victorian-era Alvan Clark Telescope. I was amazed that century-old clockworks and optics could still be used to produce cutting edge science.

Once I finished my astronomy degree, I moved to Albuquerque for a job at the University of New Mexico and I started attending the city's annual science fiction convention, Bubonicon. I was delighted to discover that Bob Vardeman was one of the local authors who attended regularly. Not only that, he was the guy who gave the convention its name! I'm glad I've had the opportunity to get to know him over the years. He's a fabulous author and I've learned a lot listening to him on panels and reading his work.

After two years in Albuquerque, my astronomy career pulled me to Tucson and then to Las Cruces. In spite of that, I've returned most years to attend Bubonicon. Even as my astronomy career progressed, I continued to work on my writing. I retained an interest in Victorian-era technology from my time at Maria Mitchell Observatory and I often worked it into my stories. Over the years I sold things like a story about airships hunting dragons to *Realms of Fantasy* Magazine and a story about Victorian-era Greek vampires to *Cemetery Dance*. I came to realize that many of my stories were related to a science fiction sub-genre called steampunk.

For as long as I can remember, I have loved early science fiction. As a kid, I devoured Jules Verne, H.G. Wells, and Edgar Rice Burroughs. I loved the sense of optimism they had about technology. My experience at Maria Mitchell Observatory had brought that kind of understandable, graspable technology right to my fingertips, and I saw firsthand that I could use that technology to monitor the pulsation of distant stars. Steampunk became a way for me to merge my love of science fiction with my experience from science.

This just leaves one more road to consider. When I was a kid, my family traveled. My dad loved to see sights ranging from Mesa Verde to Plymouth Rock. That love of history stayed with me and I find it impossible to ignore those stories from places I live. I brought all of these elements together in my Wild West Steampunk Adventure novel called *Owl Dance*, which tells the story of a sheriff and his girlfriend on the run from the law, while an alien begins tampering with history as we know it. I enjoyed it so much, I wrote a sequel called *Lightning Wolves*.

Since leaving Albuquerque, I have lived within 100 miles of the border between the United States and Mexico. Columbus, New Mexico—the site of Pancho Villa's 1916 raid on the United States—is less than a two-hour drive from my home in Las Cruces. In fact, a victim of that raid is buried in the cemetery just a couple of blocks from my house. Pancho Villa lore drifts in the very air of Southern New Mexico and Arizona.

So, when Bob Vardeman asked me if I'd be interested in contributing a story to a shared steampunk world called Empires of Steam and Rust, I had to say yes. There was no question the story would be related to the United States and Mexican Border. When I realized the year was 1915, I knew the story had to be about Pancho Villa. I also knew the story would be about introducing new technology into the world. The muse can be a tricky lady. Most of the time she sits quietly in the corner, doing her own thing, ignoring me even when summoned. In this case, she grabbed me by the scruff of the neck and wouldn't let me stop writing until the story was done. She even arranged a free trip to the Hotel Gadsden for a book signing so I could see the location of the story's climactic scenes first hand.

Of course, I also had to throw in a couple of cameos from the Clockwork Legion series. In *Revolution of Air and Rust* you met the engineer Onofre Cisneros. In *Owl Dance*, his life was changed by meeting Sheriff Ramon Morales and his girlfriend Fatemeh Karimi. Together, they went off and fought airships over Russia. That encounter never happened in this world. You also met Alethea Seton, who appears in *Wolf Posse*. When the new novel comes out, you'll find out that *Revolution's* Alethea has a very different fate than her Clockwork Legion counterpart!

What excites me about the Empire of Steam and Rust series is its globe-spanning nature. Already there are stories set in Europe and Russia. I gather there are stories in the works set in Japan and Northern Africa. I hope you'll join us for more Adventures in Steampunkery in the months to come. In the meantime, I'd like to whet your appetite with a sample of Bob Vardeman's first book in the series, *Gateway to Rust and Ruin*.

# Excerpt from *Gateway to Rust and Ruin*
by Robert E. Vardeman

## Chapter One

"We're going down, Kapitän!"

Kapitän Paul Rodet grabbed a stanchion to the right of the pilot as the ponderously overloaded zeppelin's nose pitched downward toward the ink black water. His pilot fought the wheel to right the mighty airship, the pride of the Kaiser's Luftwaffe. Rodet cursed the need for the *Eisen Adler* to leave its duty station on the Franco-Prussian border and take on a mission turning such a noble warship into nothing more than a lumbering aerial cargo vessel. Still, the *Eisen Adler* had made the Atlantic crossing in record time, a feat that would be appreciated only by the Kaiser and his generals of the Imperial High Command.

The zeppelin need only survive this night so he could surrender his logbook to the bureaucrats making note of such accomplishments, secret or public. There would be medals and commendations all around. It was not lost on Rodet that a staff position at the Imperial High Command might open for him, also. If the mission proved successful.

"Reverse engines full," Rodet said, trying to keep the irritation from his voice. These were battle-hardened Mannschaft, not giddy young Frauenzimmer. The day before they had embarked on the transoceanic flight, they had fought two French blimps intruding on Prussian airspace, severely damaging both and causing them to flee back to their field in Lille.

Immediately after the skirmish, it had pained him to dock the *Eisen Adler* at the Kaiser's newly seized field at Strasbourg and strip away most weapons from the mighty zeppelin. All that remained were a pair of water-cooled MG08 machine guns hardly fit for a ground-gripping soldier, much less the proud Iron Eagle. There had been room for only a few of the cloth ammunition belts each holding 250 rounds. Every kilogram mattered for both the speedy journey to America and the escape. Stinging as badly was leaving behind half his crew and running with only engine room and command deck personnel.

Every gram mattered so they could load that much more into the cargo hold.

"Full reverse!" Leutnant Bergen snapped, moving closer to the pilot. Rodet did not hear what his second in command whispered, but the pilot blanched. Discipline was easily maintained when a captain had such competent under officers. Bergen was a distant cousin of the Kaiser and intent on commanding his own zeppelin one day. Rodet had every confidence that he would. Rodet vowed, however, that Bergen would never command the *Eisen Adler*. This staunch ship was *his*. Until he wore admiral's epaulets and sat on the Imperial High Command.

The nose began rising.

"All ahead full," Rodet ordered when the bubble in the carpenter's level showed the zeppelin was almost level again. The inertia imparted by the sudden engine reversal carried the airship a little too far up nose, but he didn't care. Righting the ship and not flying too low over the lake below was paramount.

He glanced at the chart of Lake Champlain and the surrounding territory. They had flown from the secret rendezvous outside Schenectady in reasonable time, considering how burdened they were with the electrical equipment in the hold.

"Change course to a compass heading of 75 degrees." With the deck level once more, he stepped to the chart table, moved around and quickly dropped a straightedge onto the sketch he had received from the weaselly little man with the toothbrush mustache back at Strasbourg.

He knew an intelligence agent when he saw one. The Kaiser surrounded himself with the scurrying little rodents, always watching with beady eyes, ready to drive a blade into a real soldier's back should the opportunity afford itself. How this map had come into Imperial hands was not Rodet's concern. Its accuracy was. In the middle of night, the zeppelin was virtually invisible from the ground, its belly painted over with sooty black splotches. Let the Americans send up their feeble ships to attack, should they even know cargo was being smuggled from their country. Any flak from the ground anti-airship batteries would be difficult to center on his zeppelin with its black underbelly and no running lights.

He took a deep breath and let it out slowly. He had to remember the *Eisen Adler* no longer flew like an eagle but more like an iron ingot, laden with heavy cargo as it was. Worse, the pitiful weapons remaining were hardly worth manning should the Americans present an aerial challenge. He had little admiration for them, their airships or their fighting acumen. They foolishly chose the wrong side in the coming war in Europe, in spite of having strong ties to the Fatherland. Half of President Roosevelt's cabinet was of German descent, not British or French. Declaring neutrality would avail the country little when those engaged in manufacturing equipment such as weighed down his zeppelin willingly supplied it to the Kaiser.

"Clear skies ahead, Kapitän," called the lookout, eyes pressed into the eyepieces of the powerful Zeiss binoculars mounted on wood post for stability.

"On the Canadian side of the lake, there will be a beacon. Do you see it?"

"Nein, wait, ja, Kapitän! I see it. Five degrees starboard to our course."

"Make the correction, Leutnant Bergen. Head directly for the beacon at an altitude of two hundred meters."

The zeppelin swayed slightly as the engine speed changed on both sides of the main cabin and the rudder pushed aside rushing air to properly position them. Deep in the zeppelin's guts came the steady hissing of the steam engines, giving power that ordinarily would have been capable of hurtling the airship forward at thirty knots. With the load, barely ten was possible.

"Beacon directly ahead!" The lookout held out his arms and then slowly raised them over his head to indicate they were on the exact course.

This was a critical moment in the flight. Rodet took a quick bearing once more to be sure they approached the beacon along the precise line needed, then calculated their speed and position. They were still over Lake Champlain but were nearing the spot penciled onto the chart. Closer, closer.

"Kapitän Rodet, we have pursuit! Two small airships!"

He glanced up at the speaking tube. The lookout positioned

at the rear of the main gondola had spotted Americans trying to overtake them. With such a load, the *Eisen Adler* had difficulty outflying a ruptured duck.

"Type?" he called into the speaking tube.

"Dirigibles. Pah, balloons!"

Such contempt would have been his, also, if they had their usual battery of weapons. Not now.

"We have been spotted by their border patrol," he said to those on deck. Ordinarily he would have enjoyed a skirmish like that in the offing. Boasting of it to his little Gisele made her proud of her papa. And Freddy, no longer little Friedrich, so soon to enter the Imperial Air Academy, would have tales to impress his squadron mates. Marta would have clucked her tongue and chided him for filling their children›s heads with such dangerous talk, but he knew she had taken pride in his exploits. Hadn't she kissed the Iron Cross he had won at Rotterdam after the Kaiser himself had pinned it to his chest?

He touched the spot where the medal had been bestowed. Only Luftwaffe insignia marked that spot now, but in the pocket under his tunic rode a picture of his lovely wife. His fingers pressed down on it as if she would respond with a smile and another kiss, then lightly caressed before turning back to completing his mission.

Rodet stared hard at the chart and pressed his finger down on a faint line of penciled dots. It was a shame his Marta had died from the French influenza. Even she, a pacifist at heart, would be proud of him when he received the new medals from the Kaiser for this mission.

"Left engines reverse," he ordered. The zeppelin's superstructure groaned under the strain of making a complete reversal in course. "Lookout, what do you see?"

"Nothing, Kapitän!"

Rodet watched the compass as the mighty airship turned.

"There, Kapitän, I see both American ships. Do I man the guns?"

"Stay at your station," Rodet snapped. "We are toothless and cannot fight, even those two worthless gas bags lofted by the Americans. You must look for the hole, as instructed."

"How can I see a hole in empty air?" complained the lookout.

"He has a point, Herr Kapitän," Bergen said in a low voice. "This makes no sense. We should prepare to repel the blimps and then escape into Canada." He glanced at the chart where Rodet's index finger still pressed down so hard that it bent slightly into a gnarled arch.

"We do not go to Canada. They would turn us over to the Americans as smugglers or perhaps spies."

"But the beacon!"

"Was there only for us to find … it." Rodet wasn't sure he believed everything he had been told in the briefing, but Luftkommandant Talmann had been adamant about the information. Rodet would follow Talmann to the gates of hell. Still, the weasel of an intelligence officer's smile had been one of satisfaction, as if he avenged some loss caused by the Luftwaffe. Rodet would have felt better if the Luftkommandant had personally given him the chart with the barely discernible pencil dots on it.

Rodet had doubted such a thing could exist, but Talmann claimed to have proof. Several peculiar portals had been found and explored. From the far side, the sky had appeared open, the beacon visible. Turning the zeppelin to face the thin air they had just traversed showed not the pursuing blimps but … nothing.

Rodet pushed aside the lookout and peered through the binoculars. As the *Eisen Adler* came about, he saw that the Luftkommandant had not lied. The running lights on the pursuing American blimps simply vanished. By careful study, he saw the occluding circular hole in thin air. It had not been visible as they followed the beacon and had passed through the spot where it hung like a siege balloon without tethers, but now that he could look back along their course, he saw … nothing.

"All stop!" he bellowed. Bergen passed along the command and the mighty engines ceased hammering at the cold atmosphere above the lake. The zeppelin drifted slightly off the proper heading, taking them out of position for entry into—through—the hole in midair.

"What is it, Kapitän?" Bergen's eyes were wide as he lowered his own binoculars and turned to his commander.

"I wish we could be sure," Rodet said in a low voice.

"Runnels, it is time for you to man the machine gun."

"Jawohl," the lookout said, snapping to attention and saluting, before diving down a trapdoor into the forward turret.

Rodet shouted after him, "Fire ten rounds!"

From the turret just below the command deck and at the front of the *Eisen Adler* came the sounds of the Maschinengewehr being loaded with its pitifully small 7.92mm rounds. A metallic click sounded as the cocking lever came back and then a short stutter as invisible rounds tore into the black hole.

"Tracers! Fire three bursts marked with tracers!"

The command was relayed to the gunner. Rodet watched the eye-searing magnesium rounds vanish into the blackness, swallowed completely in a hidden giant's maw.

"We are to fly *there?*" Bergen asked.

"We will. For honor and duty, we will!" Rodet sucked in his breath and then released it slowly, ready to give the order.

"We're hit! The blimps have opened fire, and they hit the port side lateral bag! We're leaking gas!"

Rodet scowled and crammed a rubber stopper into the speaking tube that was blaring such unwanted reports. He could not be distracted now and did not want any of the command deck personnel to be, either.

A hydrogen leak wasn't fatal. What might be were the unseen attacking blimps if they continued such accurate—or lucky—fire. They were hidden by the hole that obliterated all light. The blimps could see the zeppelin from the far side and fire at them, but Rodet could not see his attackers. Worse, the rounds from his tiny gun arched rounds into emptiness, not a solid target. Like an American patrol blimp.

"All engines, full speed ahead. Five degrees starboard rudder."

He heard Bergen gasp, then relay the orders to the pilot and engine room. The mighty props began turning, slowly at first, then with more power to drive the zeppelin ahead. To the attacking blimps it must seem that the *Eisen Adler* sailed directly into their guns. Despair filled the zeppelin's captain as the ship centered on the black hole and then slid forward.

What did it look like to the blimps? He couldn't say since the nose of the zeppelin suddenly looked as if it had been cut off. Then the zeppelin slid into the void within a void and blackness cloaked him and the control deck. He shivered although he felt no chill. The banked lights in his zeppelin never flickered, but their light failed to escape even a few inches. Rodet pulled away the baffle from a lamp overhead. The light cast a warm yellow glow on everything inside. Beyond the glass windows of the gondola, the light simply vanished.

"Kapitän, I cannot see." Bergen's voice cracked with fear.

"Full speed ahead, Leutnant. Maintain this heading. Do not veer from it one degree. On your life, not a half degree! We have been given orders by the Imperial Command and assured we will bring glory to the Fatherland with our heroics this day!"

Rodet wished he believed that. He pressed the eyepieces hard into his face and stared ahead. Nothing. From the sides of encroaching blackness he saw fleeting movement, indistinct and distant. Then he cried out in joy as a spot of light appeared ahead.

"We're coming through the other side! The Alps. Those are the Alps in daylight!"

Rodet's triumph died as the *Eisen Adler* was cut in half. Robbed of its lift from the prodigious bags of hydrogen, the airship gondola angled downward, gathered speed and smashed into the ground. Rodet died with a curse on his lips for Talmann, the Imperial High Command and even Kaiser Wilhelm but his final thoughts were of his children and that he would join his dear Marta too soon.

Continued in *Gateway to Rust and Ruin*
by Robert E. Vardeman.
Available at your favorite ebook vendor!

Also available in the Empires of Steam and Rust series:
*Heart of Steam and Rust* by Stephen D. Sullivan
*Unforeseen: Journey Through Rust and Ruin* by Sarah Bartsch